CLAUDIA'S BIG PARTY

**Other books by
Ann M. Martin**

P.S. Longer Letter Later
(written with Paula Danziger)
Leo the Magnificat
Rachel Parker, Kindergarten Show-off
Eleven Kids, One Summer
Ma and Pa Dracula
Yours Turly, Shirley
Ten Kids, No Pets
Slam Book
Just a Summer Romance
Missing Since Monday
With You and Without You
Me and Katie (the Pest)
Stage Fright
Inside Out
Bummer Summer

THE KIDS IN MS. COLMAN'S CLASS series
BABY-SITTERS LITTLE SISTER series
THE BABY-SITTERS CLUB mysteries
THE BABY-SITTERS CLUB series
CALIFORNIA DIARIES series

CLAUDIA'S BIG PARTY

Ann M. Martin

AN
APPLE
PAPERBACK

SCHOLASTIC INC.
New York Toronto London Auckland Sydney

Cover art by Hodges Soileau

No part of this publication may be reproduced in whole or in part, or stored in a retrieval system, or transmitted in any form or by any means, electronic, mechanical, photocopying, recording, or otherwise, without written permission of the publisher. For information regarding permission, write to Scholastic Inc., Attention: Permissions Department, 555 Broadway, New York, NY 10012.

ISBN 0-590-50174-7

12 11 10 9 8 7 6 5 4 3 2 1   8 9/9 0 1 2 3/0

Printed in the U.S.A.   40

First Scholastic printing, October 1998

The author gratefully acknowledges
Vicki Berger Erwin
for her help in
preparing this manuscript.

CHAPTER 1

"Claudia! Why are you cleaning out your locker *now*? It's Friday. School's out for the weekend. And we're going S-H-O-P-P-I-N-G." Joanna Fried sang the letters of the last word as she, Shira Epstein, and Jeannie Kim swooped down on me.

S-H-O-P-P-I-N-G. Two *P*'s? Joanna would know better than I, the world's biggest enemy of the spelled word. Although you'd think I'd know how to spell one of my favorite activities.

"Earrings," said Jeannie, "to go with this vest." She modeled her black velour vest, pointing out the red ribbon roses decorating the bottom edge. With her black jeans, black suede shoes, and long-sleeved white shirt, it made a very cool outfit.

"Dangly red roses?" I leaned forward to look at the vest a little more closely. If we found matching red ribbon, I might be able to make Jeannie some earrings. As I leaned over, I shrugged my overstuffed backpack to the ground. The sound of at least a hundred pounds of books hitting the floor made people turn around and look.

"It's not an earthquake," Joanna assured the crowd in the hallway, "only Claudia's backpack."

Shira burst into giggles, which spread to the rest of us.

"What is in there?" Jeannie asked. "Explosives?"

"Homework," I explained.

Shira stopped laughing, and her blue eyes grew to the size of small plates. "Eighth grade means that much homework?"

"It does for me," I said to my seventh-grade friends. And they understood. They know me pretty well, even though we haven't been friends all that long. I'd been a year ahead of them in school until recently. And I'd always had to dog-paddle like crazy just to keep my head above water in all my subjects — except art, which happens to be my best subject and my favorite. My teachers, parents, and counselors came up with a plan that involved my going back to seventh grade to catch up. I did and found out that school wasn't as hard as I'd thought. And, it wasn't long before I did so well that I was offered the chance to move back to eighth grade. I took it. But not before I picked up an entire group of new friends, plus a boyfriend, Josh Rocker, who was walking toward us just then, as if my thoughts had summoned him.

Suddenly I realized I had made plans to hang out with Josh. Somehow that had slipped my mind. "Oh, wow," I exclaimed, "I totally forgot!" I knelt beside my bag and tried to stuff in one more book. No matter how I arranged and rearranged them, only four of the five I needed would fit.

"Totally forgot what?" Josh knelt beside me and tugged on the book I was still holding. I let go, and he ended up sitting down unexpectedly in the middle of the hall. All of us, including Josh, laughed again. "I was going to do that to you," he said, standing up and brushing off the seat of his jeans.

"I beat you to it." I smiled at him, glad to see him after a long day.

Josh flashed me a grin and tucked my book under his arm. "You ready?"

I looked at Jeannie, Joanna, and Shira standing on one side of me and Josh standing on the other. Then I looked at my watch and calculated how much time was left before I had to be at my Baby-sitters Club meeting — and came up with, well, not enough to shop with my friends, *and* hang out with Josh. The BSC meets at my house every Monday, Wednesday, and Friday afternoon at five-thirty (more about this later). The club members are close friends of mine too. Sometimes I feel as though I need two or three more of me to be able to spend enough time with all my friends.

"Ready for what?" Joanna asked.

Josh looked from me to the girls, his smile fading. "Claudia? We have plans, right?"

I nodded.

"But you said you were going shopping with us!" Shira said.

I nodded again.

"No problem," said Joanna. "You can come shopping with us, Josh." Joanna, who's super-organized (she's president of the seventh-grade class), always has an answer. She grabbed my math book out of my backpack and headed for the door.

I turned to Josh, not saying anything but trying to communicate with my eyes how much I wanted him to say he'd go. He looked at the floor for a second, then nodded, the grin back in place. I felt like giving him a hug. And I knew he wouldn't mind going shopping with us. He did it all the time before we were boyfriend and girlfriend. He likes Joanna, Shira, and Jeannie as much as I do.

My backpack with only three books in it was much easier to handle than my backpack with five books in it. I knew Mom, Dad, and my sister, Janine, had plans for working with me this weekend. Studying and my homework had been a pretty important part of our family life since I returned to the eighth grade. Academics really matter to my family. Dad is a partner in an investment firm in Stamford, Connecticut (a larger town than Stoneybrook, where we live). He can't wait until I study stocks and bonds, but for now he's a big help in social studies. Mom is the head librarian at the Stoneybrook Public Library and sometimes I think she knows about everything! Then there's Janine. She's sixteen and a junior at Stoneybrook High School, but she takes classes at Stoneybrook University. She lives for homework, her own as well as mine. It all seems to come pretty easily to her. She's a genius with the IQ to prove it.

Sometimes I look at them sitting around the table, talking about computers or astronomy or some book they've all read, and I wonder how I ended up in this family. We *look* like a family, though — a Japanese-American family. And they're incredibly supportive of me. I love art (creating it as well as appreciating it), fashion, junk food, and Nancy Drew mysteries. My family likes art too, but to look at only. As for the rest . . . it's an understatement to say that they don't approve. (That's why junk food and Nancy Drew books are *hidden* all over my room.)

Josh walked behind the rest of us. I looked

over my shoulder and found him staring at me. I slowed my pace to walk alongside him. "Are you okay with this?" I asked. He shrugged, but he was smiling.

Shira turned around and, walking backward, asked me about eighth grade. "So how much homework is there regularly?"

Shira's hair practically glittered in the bright sunlight. Tall and skinny, she towers over the rest of us. She worries a lot more than the rest of us too.

"It's not that bad," I assured her. "You won't have a bit of trouble." Shira executed a little skip-turn, satisfied with my answers. Jeannie and Joanna won't have any trouble either. They're both smart and do well in school. They have trouble believing that I have to work as hard as I do in eighth grade, since I used to help them when we studied together for our seventh-grade classes. It's a little easier the second time around.

On our way downtown, we had to stop at Shira's house, so she could get some money. Then we stopped at Joanna's house, so she could set her VCR for a show she needed to tape. By the time we were ready to shop, it was nearly four o'clock.

"Where do you want to go first?" Jeannie asked as we finally approached downtown Stoneybrook.

I knew she wanted to go to the Merry-Go-Round and shop for earrings. I wanted to stop by the thrift shop to see what they'd added recently. That's one of the differences between Jeannie and me, although we both like clothes. I like to put together different outfits from what I have, what I can make, and what I buy here and there. Consignment stores are places for me to treasure hunt. Some of the best outfits I've ever put together come from things I've picked up secondhand. I have a policy of never wearing the same outfit twice — even if that means changing only a scarf or the earrings I'd worn before. Jeannie, who is also Asian-American, likes to wear the kinds of outfits you'd see on a mannequin or in *Twist* magazine.

Josh might want to go to the music store, but he wasn't saying much. Shira and Joanna were leaning toward the Merry-Go-Round.

"Is that okay?" I asked Josh. He shrugged again. "You aren't saying a whole lot. Is everything all right?" Josh is usually in the middle of any conversation, no matter what the topic.

"I'm fine," he said.

I wasn't convinced. We turned into the store and crowded around the earring counter.

"Look for red roses," Shira directed, walking around the counter slowly.

I let my backpack slip off my shoulders. It didn't make nearly as much noise this time, but we all giggled again when it hit the floor.

Except Josh. He wore a puzzled look. "What?" he asked.

"Earlier I dropped my backpack and it was so full, it made this huge noise," I tried to explain. It didn't sound very funny. It was one of those things that you had to have been there for to understand. Josh's mouth turned up at the corners for a quick moment, then his eyebrows collided as he frowned.

I decided to stay close to him. "What do you think about those?" I asked, pointing to a pair of earrings I'd just spotted. They were tiny paintbrushes made out of real bristles, with a different color of paint on the tip of each one. I like to make my own earrings, but I'm not above buying them if they're creative enough.

"Umm," Josh answered.

"Joanna!" I'd caught a glimpse of the perfect pair for Ms. President — a pair of gavels. They weren't a reserved presidential gold or silver, though. They were made of rainbow-striped plastic. I couldn't imagine anyone but Joanna wearing them. "These have your name written all over them."

Joanna leaned across the counter. "That's not how you spell Joanna," she said, the glass case steaming up as her breath hit it.

"It's how you spell president," I said.

"May I see that pair, please?" Joanna asked

the clerk, tapping on the glass above the gavels.

The salesclerk, a girl I thought I recognized as someone in Janine's class at SHS, opened the case and handed the card with the gavel earrings to Joanna.

"While you have that open, could I please see the paintbrushes?" I asked, pointing them out.

"I'd like to see the gold roses and the red roses, please," Jeannie said from her place at the counter.

"And the books and those big blue globes for me, please," Shira added.

The clerk sighed, pulling out all the earrings we'd asked to see. "How about you?" she said to Josh.

He backed away, shaking his head and holding his hand in front of him.

"Come on, Josh," said Jeannie. "Claudia will hold your hand while someone here pierces your ear."

"Both of them, if you want," said Shira.

"Hold both his hands or pierce both his ears?" Joanna asked.

I turned toward Josh, smiling, ready to say I'd be glad to hold both his hands. But he wasn't smiling.

"No thanks," he said, turning his back and walking to a rack of key chains.

Shira frowned, as if she realized she'd gone a little too far.

I started to follow Josh, but before I'd taken two steps, Jeannie called me back. "What do you think, fashion guru? Are these roses too different from the ones on the vest?"

I glanced back, thinking I'd be able to answer with a quick yes or no and join Josh, but I wanted to be sure, which meant I had to look closer. "Not the gold ones," I said. "Too bright. Hold the red roses up to your ears."

Jeannie shook back her long hair and held one earring to each ear. They were exactly right for the outfit. The roses were a little smaller than the ones on the vest, but they were a close match in color and style. "Perfect!" I said.

"I can't believe how different roses can look," said Jeannie, pushing the earrings across the counter to the clerk and nodding that she wanted to buy them. "These are kind of flat and these are huge." She showed me at least a dozen pairs of rose earrings on display.

Shira was trying the blue globes. "You have to buy those," Joanna urged her. "They are the exact same color as your eyes!"

I had to check that out too.

"Next time I have to conduct a class meeting, no one will be able to look away if I wear these," Joanna decided, admiring the gavel earrings.

10

"You might even be able to use them to call the meeting to order," Jeannie joked. "They're big enough."

Shira asked me about a second pair of earrings, then Joanna called to me to see some hair clips.

When I finally looked around to find Josh, I caught a glimpse of the large Winnie-the-Pooh clock hanging on the wall. I couldn't believe how much time had passed. If I didn't leave soon, I was going to be late for the BSC meeting.

"You guys, I have to go! It's almost time for my meeting." I picked up my backpack and with a groan slung it over my shoulder.

"Don't forget this one." Joanna handed over the book she'd carried for me.

"Don't forget me," Josh mumbled, just loud enough for me to hear. He held out the book *he'd* carried.

"Josh, I'm really sorry. I thought we'd be finished here quickly and then you and I could — "

"Have some quality time?" he interrupted.

"That's what I thought," I said in a low voice. "Are you mad?"

Josh shook his head. "Ask me if I'm disappointed."

"Are you disappointed?"

"Are you?"

11

I nodded. "What if I call you tonight, after dinner?"

A big smile spread across Josh's face, the smile I like to think of as "my" smile. "I could live with that," he said.

"Okay, it's a date. And speaking of dates, don't forget about tomorrow night — you, me, Logan, Mary Anne, Stacey, and Ethan," I said, walking quickly toward the door.

"How could I forget?" Josh called after me.

Something in the way he said it made me think he wasn't excited. But maybe that was my imagination.

CHAPTER 2

The front door was unlocked. We always leave it that way on days the BSC meets. I threw it open and ran up the steps.

Kristy Thomas looked up from the clipboard she was holding. "Hi. Where've you been?" she asked. She was sitting in the same place she always sits during our meetings — in my director's chair — and she had stuck a pencil behind her ear. Mary Anne Spier was already there too, sitting on my bed.

"Shopping," I replied breathlessly. I dropped my backpack in the middle of the floor, feeling as if I might never move my shoulders again. After throwing the other two books on my bed, I stretched my arms toward the ceiling and rolled my shoulders.

"Buy a lot?" Kristy asked, staring at the backpack.

"Nope. Books," I replied, making a face.

Kristy nodded. Luckily, my BSC friends understood my situation. I'd worried that when I moved to seventh grade, things might change. Staying close to somebody who's in a different grade, or goes to a different school, can be difficult. But they stuck by me all the way. I guess that's one good test of friendship.

So what's the BSC all about? I'll start at the beginning. Kristy, of the director's chair and pencil, is the founder and president. One afternoon, back in seventh grade, she watched her mother trying to find a baby-sitter for her little brother, David Michael — calling one sitter, being turned down, hanging up, and calling the next sitter on her list. Like a lightning bolt, it hit Kristy. Wouldn't it be easier to find a sitter if there was one number you could call to reach several people at once? That's the idea behind the BSC.

As I mentioned earlier we meet every Monday, Wednesday, and Friday afternoon from five-thirty (on the dot) until six, in my room. (I'm the only one in the club with a private phone on a separate line. That's what landed me the job of vice-president.) Parents call and request a sitter. The person who answers the phone takes down the information about the job — what time, how many kids, and so on. Then we figure out which of us can take it and call the client back to tell him or her who will be coming.

14

The BSC is as much a business as it is a club, and Kristy keeps the business humming. She's constantly coming up with new ideas to improve the way we work. For example, it was her idea to have a club notebook, in which each of us writes about every job we take. This is one of my least favorite club activities. I love the jobs, but writing about them is a different story. Still, I like to read what everyone else writes, and it's very helpful to know what's going on with all of the kids for whom we baby-sit.

Kristy also invented Kid-Kits. Those are cardboard boxes filled with books, hand-me-down toys, and other supplies we sometimes take with us on jobs. We each decorate our own and customize the contents. Mine, for example, has a lot of art materials in it. Kid-Kits are very useful on rainy days, with new clients, and when something new or different is going on in a family.

The one thing that Kristy seldom has a new idea about is her clothes. Just as she sits in the same place at every BSC meeting, she wears a variation of the same outfit just about every day. Kristy's closets and drawers are full of jeans, T-shirts, turtlenecks, and running shoes.

Kristy used to live across the street from me on Bradford Court. She'd lived there forever with her mother and her three brothers, Charlie, Sam, and David Michael. Charlie and Sam are in high school, and David Michael is a second-grader. Mr. Thomas left the family when David Michael was just a baby. Kristy hears from him every now and then. Not long ago, the Thomases made a big move — to a mansion across town. Why? Her family suddenly needed more room. Mrs. Thomas married a really nice guy named Watson Brewer, who happens to be a millionaire with a house big enough for all of them. "All of them" means the extra people who came along with Watson: Karen and Andrew, Watson's children from his first marriage, live with them in alternate months. And after Watson and Kristy's mom were married, the Brewers adopted Emily Michelle, a two-and-a-half-year-old who was born in Vietnam. Then Kristy's grandmother, Nannie, moved in to help. Plenty of pets share the house too — maybe enough to fill a small kennel.

Food! I needed food. I found a bag of M&M's in my desk drawer, ripped it open, and poured out a handful. Yum! Chocolate helped. I passed the bag to Kristy, who was talking quietly with Mary Anne. One of my duties as vice-president of the BSC is to make sure everyone is fed. And that's no problem because I keep a "healthy" supply of junk food (and other food).

When Kristy came up with the idea for the

BSC, she asked Mary Anne and me to join it. Back then, Mary Anne also lived on Bradford Court, next door to Kristy. They've been best friends practically since they were born. Mary Anne's mother died when Mary Anne was a baby, so for a long time her family was just her and her dad. Mr. Spier was pretty strict. He made rules for Mary Anne about how she had to dress, how she could wear her hair, and how late she could stay out. It wasn't easy for Mary Anne — she's one of the shyest, most sensitive people I know — but she stood up to her dad and he loosened up a little. Mary Anne cut her brown hair, bought some new clothes, and was given the same curfew the rest of us had.

Then even bigger changes took place in her family. Mary Anne made a new friend, Dawn Schafer, who had moved to Stoneybrook from California. Together they found out that their parents, Mary Anne's widowed father and Dawn's divorced mother, had dated in high school. They did some matchmaking and before long Mary Anne had a new stepmother, Sharon; a new stepsister (and best friend), Dawn; and a new stepbrother, Jeff. Mary Anne, Mr. Spier, and Tigger (Mary Anne's kitten) moved into the Schafers' old farmhouse, and began life as a blended family. After awhile, Dawn decided to return to California and live with her dad. (Jeff had already made that move.) That means Mary Anne and Dawn are long-distance sisters now, but they're still close. They talk on the phone and visit whenever they can, but they miss each other a lot. When Dawn lived here, she was a BSC member too. She's our honorary member now. When she visits, it's as if she's never been gone.

Mary Anne is the BSC secretary. She's in charge of the club record book, where we keep track of all our schedules, clients' names and addresses, ages of the kids for whom we baby-sit, rates we charge, and any other special information about the children. She's the perfect person for the job because she's very organized (and she knows how to spell).

Mary Anne used to be the only one of us with a steady boyfriend. His name is Logan Bruno. Now I'm seeing Josh, and Stacey McGill, another BSC member who's also my best friend, has an "older" boyfriend from New York City, Ethan Carroll. The following night the six of us were going on our first triple date, and I couldn't wait.

"Did you buy anything this afternoon?" Stacey asked, as she moved my books aside and sat down on the bed next to me. Mallory Pike and Jessi Ramsey had come in with her. They sat on the floor, looking at a book Jessi held on her lap.

"Not one single thing," I answered. I hadn't

even had time to try on the paintbrush ear-rings. I dug around in my desk a little more, pulled out some pretzels, and handed them to Stacey. I keep a special stash of healthier snacks for Stacey because she can't eat sugary junk food. Stacey has diabetes, a condition that interferes with the way her body processes sugar. If she eats certain things, she can become very sick. As long as Stacey is very careful about her diet, monitors her blood sugar level, and gives herself daily injections of insulin, she's fine. But it's something she'll have to deal with her whole life.

Stacey moved to Stoneybrook from New York City when we were in seventh grade, and we invited her to join the BSC not long after she arrived. Stacey is tall, thin, blonde, and beautiful. Like me, she loves fashion, but her look is more grown-up and sophisticated than mine — or anyone else's in the BSC. It's the New York influence. Stacey moved back to New York after she'd lived here awhile. Then her parents divorced, and she and her mother moved back to Stoneybrook. Stacey's dad still lives in New York City, and she visits there often. That's how she met Ethan.

Math is one of Stacey's strong points, so naturally she's our BSC treasurer. She collects dues from us every Monday. We use the money to pay Charlie for driving Kristy and (usually)

Abby Stevenson to our meetings, to pay for part of my phone bill, to buy supplies for our Kid-Kits, and to fund special events for our charges. Sometimes, when we have a little extra money in the treasury, we spend it on a pizza party.

Kristy looked at my digital clock. It read 5:29. Just then, Abby burst into the room.

"I'm not late, am I?" Abby said, breathing hard.

Kristy stared at Abby for a moment. "Nope." When the clock clicked over to 5:30, she said, "The meeting will come to order."

Abby sank to the floor, then stretched her legs out in front of her. She leaned forward, touching her face to her knees. I'd seen Jessi do that lots of time, but never Abby. "What?" she asked as she straightened up and found all of us staring at her. "I need to cool down. I ran today, but I'm a little off. I should have made it here with more time to spare." She continued to stretch.

Abby is our newest BSC member. She recently moved to Stoneybrook from Long Island with her mother and her sister, Anna. They live on Kristy's street. Abby and Anna are identical twins. They have totally different interests, though. Abby loves sports and outdoor activities, while Anna is a serious musician. We invited both Abby and Anna to join the BSC, but

20

Anna decided she wouldn't have time to baby-sit *and* practice the violin as much as she likes. Abby is our alternate officer, which means she takes over the duties of any club officer who might be absent. She has asthma and is allergic to a long list of foods and other stuff, but she doesn't let any of that slow her down for a moment. Abby's dad died in a car accident when she was nine. She doesn't talk much about it, but it must be hard. Losing people you love is always difficult. I know because my grandmother, Mimi, died not long ago. She lived with us, and we were very close. I still miss her.

The phone rang almost as soon as Kristy called the meeting to order. Stacey answered, and the BSC was open for business.

Jessi and Mallory continued to pore over the book. They're our junior officers, and they're best friends. Both are in sixth grade and can only baby-sit in the afternoons unless it's for their own siblings. They share a love of horses and books, and each is the oldest kid in her family. So they have plenty in common. By the way, there are eight children in Mal's family, four girls and four boys, including identical triplets. There are three kids in Jessi's family.

"Mal, you're free Thursday afternoon. Want to baby-sit for the Rodowskys?" Mary Anne asked after checking the schedules in the record book.

When Mal looked up, I noticed the dark circles under her eyes. She shook her head, her reddish-brown curls swinging, then buried her face in the book again.

Stacey and I exchanged glances. Things hadn't been going well for Mal lately. Not long ago some of the crueler kids in school started calling her "Spaz Girl." I'd hoped it would blow over, but the nickname spread through the entire school. Maybe this experience will find its way into a book someday. That's what Mal wants to do — write and illustrate children's books.

Mal is lucky to have Jessi as a friend to help her through this. They've been friends since Jessi's first day of school in Stoneybrook. (The Ramseys moved here from Oakley, New Jersey.) In addition to the interest in books and horses she shares with Mal, Jessi loves dancing. She studies ballet seriously and is very talented. She even looks like a dancer — tall and graceful, with her black hair often pulled back from her face in a bun. Jessi has a younger sister, Becca, and a baby brother, John Philip, Jr., better known as Squirt.

There are two other members of the BSC, associate members who don't regularly attend meetings but who handle our overflow jobs. One is Shannon Kilbourne, the only one of us who doesn't attend Stoneybrook Middle

School. She goes to Stoneybrook Day School. Shannon lives on Kristy and Abby's street. She's very involved in activities at her school, so she doesn't have time left for any more regular meetings.

Finally, there's Logan, who, as I mentioned, is Mary Anne's boyfriend. He's cute, with blondish-brown curly hair and blue eyes. He's also funny, and wonderfully understanding, and he has the greatest southern accent. Logan used to live in Louisville, Kentucky, and you can still hear it in his voice.

"What time are we meeting tomorrow night?" Mary Anne asked Stacey and me. "Logan has a football game in the afternoon and he needs time to clean up before we go out."

"I'd hope so!" said Stacey. "Ethan is coming in on the four-fifteen train from New York. Mom and I are going to pick him up at the station, then take him back to the house. We might drive around town too, since Ethan's never been here."

"Are you nervous?" I asked. Stacey was twisting her blonde hair around her finger, something she doesn't often do.

"A little," she admitted.

I understood. Ethan is fifteen and the rest of us are thirteen, except Josh, who is still twelve. "We won't embarrass you, will we, Mary Anne?"

"You won't and I won't. I can't speak for Logan or Josh," she said, smiling.

"Josh is looking forward to going out with all of you," I said. I hoped. "I'll talk to him tonight and make sure he knows what's expected of him."

"Don't do that! You don't want to make him nervous. Josh is fun. He'll be fine. And so will Logan. It's just that Ethan is used to New York and we're in Stoneybrook," Stacey pointed out.

"We're adjourned — " The phone interrupted Kristy's announcement. She reached out and picked up the receiver. "Baby-sitters Club," she said. "Yes, it's Kristy, Mrs. Korman. . . . I'll check the schedule and call you back to tell you who your sitter will be. Thanks for calling." Kristy dropped the receiver back into the cradle. "Who's available to sit for the Kormans tomorrow afternoon? Bill and Melody only. Mr. and Mrs. Korman are taking Skylar to a special baby gym class."

I waited for someone else to speak up. I was free, but between the pile of homework waiting for me and the big date tomorrow night, I wasn't sure I had time.

"I'll take it," Abby volunteered. "And I'll even call Mrs. Korman to tell her."

"Do you want to ride home, or are you running?" Kristy asked as Abby dialed the Kormans' number and everyone else prepared to leave.

"Mrs. Korman? What?" Abby held the phone to one ear and clamped her free hand over the other. "It's Abby Stevenson. I'm available to baby-sit for you tomorrow." She listened, then repeated, "What? . . . Okay, see you then." Abby hung up, shaking her head. "Whoa! Sounds like a war zone at the Kormans'. Melody was crying and Bill was yelling. I could barely hear a word Mrs. Korman said. I hope they reach some kind of truce by tomorrow afternoon."

CHAPTER 3

I looked at the telephone sitting on my night-stand. Janine was checking the math problems I'd managed to finish in the hour we'd been working together. I still had six to go, but I wanted to make sure I was doing them correctly before I went any further. If it was going to take her awhile, maybe I could sneak in a call to Josh. My parents had made it a rule that I had to finish at least some of my weekend homework on Friday. In the past, I'd had a habit of leaving everything until Sunday night and then feeling as if I couldn't face it because there was so much. I wasn't technically finished with what I needed to do tonight, but I *had* done a fair amount.

I stood up, stretched, and took three steps toward the telephone.

Janine's head snapped up. "Where are you going?"

"I need to call Josh and tell him what time

we're going out tomorrow night," I said.

"Claudia, you're aware of the restrictions on your use of the telephone before you complete your homework assignments," Janine reminded me.

I rolled my eyes. Janine sometimes talks as if she's choosing words out of a special genius dictionary, especially when the subject is schoolwork.

"There are a few principles in this assignment that need further clarification. Come sit here and we'll discuss the issues that are contributing to your errors." Janine patted the seat of my desk chair. "Don't be discouraged. You're doing an admirable job, especially in light of the fact that this concept was only recently introduced. Your errors may simply be a matter of too little attention to detail."

Something I'm sure my sister would never be guilty of. I sat down. "Don't you have anything better to do than help me with math on a Friday night? I could have started with history or English. Mom and Dad offered to work with me." Looking at Janine's face, I felt bad for asking that question. She'd broken up with her boyfriend, Jerry Michaels, recently. Even though it had been Janine's idea, they'd gone out for a long time, so I'm sure it wasn't easy.

"I don't mind spending the evening with my sister." Janine smiled and pushed her glasses up on her nose. "Jerry was a person whose presence in my life expanded geometrically rather than arithmetically, taking up more time than one person should."

I nodded, not quite sure what she meant, but realizing, now that I thought about it, that she used to spend more time with Jerry than with anyone else. I thought of Josh again. I wished I had more time to spend with him. But as Janine might say, time is a constant. There's only a certain amount of it.

"How about adding a little $C_{12}H_{22}O_{11}$ to this equation?" Janine asked.

I leaned over and looked at my math paper. "Which one?"

Janine laughed. "$C_{12}H_{22}O_{11}$ is the chemical compound for sucrose. The main component of your . . . junk food."

"You want some candy?" I asked. Janine can be so weird. Why didn't she just say candy?

"What kind do you have?"

"Snickers." I opened the middle drawer in my desk, reached to the back, and found two candy bars.

"Thank you." Janine unwrapped hers and began to nibble.

"So, what have I done wrong here?" I asked, with my mouth full of chocolate, peanuts, caramel, and nougat.

"How is Josh Rocker fitting into the equation of your life?" Janine replied.

I was so surprised I stopped chewing and my mouth fell open. I'm sure it looked charming, since it was full of candy bar. I swallowed. The equation of my life was kind of out of balance at the moment, but Janine probably wouldn't be interested in that. "Josh is fun," I said.

"Fun is important," she replied, nodding.

Even I, with my normal IQ, knew that. I also knew that the sooner we finished the math, the sooner I could call Josh. I stared at the small check marks Janine had made in several places.

"The first three problems are perfect," she said.

I took a moment to enjoy my success. Janine continued, explaining the errors I'd made in the other problems. Most of them were from working too quickly, I realized. I erased the wrong answers. "Let me finish these problems and you'll be free," I said, bending over my paper. It didn't take me long.

"Janine?" She'd stood up while I was working. I turned in my chair to see her standing in front of my dresser, holding a pair of feather earrings up to her ears.

"What do you think?" she asked, turning around.

"Hmmm," was my enthusiastic response. Not in a million years could I imagine my sister going out in public in feather earrings. She tended to wear tiny gold balls and pearl studs, when she bothered with earrings at all. "I'm finished correcting the problems. I'll work on the rest of the assignment while you're checking these."

"Maybe then we could bake cookies together?"

Again I looked at Janine.

"We seldom indulge in any activities together beyond math homework, Claudia. It might be fun."

Janine looked so hopeful. Did she truly want to be with *me*, or was she lonely? Oh, well. Maybe I could sneak in a telephone call to Josh while the cookies were baking.

I was about to agree when there was a knock on the door. "May we come in?" Mom asked.

I quickly shoved our candy wrappers in my math book.

"Sorry to interrupt your study session," Dad said as he and Mom stepped into my room. They looked around, and I could almost hear what they were thinking. I tend to be creative in my room decor too — clothes draped over furniture and on the floor, the bedspread artistically wrinkled.

"Something has come up," Mom began.

Janine and I sat up a little straighter. Mom looked awfully serious.

"It's good news," she added, her eyes sparkling. "I think."

"Tell us," I said.

Mom pulled and patted the bedspread, removing the wrinkles. Then she and Dad sat down facing us.

"The news is good for me, anyway," Mom began. "I've been invited to attend a library convention in Chicago."

"That's wonderful," Janine put in. "Is it the one you mentioned last summer? There were some speakers you were anxious to hear."

Mom nodded. "Yes. The representative from our region, southern Connecticut, has to have back surgery and won't be able to attend. He asked me to go in his place. So it isn't good news for Mr. Christian." She looked at Dad. "But I guess it is for me."

"The convention is next weekend," Dad continued. "You may remember Jim Simpson, who used to work at the firm with me. He and his family moved to Chicago and we haven't seen him in several years. Your mom and I thought this might be the perfect opportunity to visit the Simpsons." He cleared his throat.

I didn't remember Jim Simpson, but Janine was nodding, so maybe she did. Chicago has a wonderful art museum and a science museum

Janine would probably love. Would we miss any school? "It sounds great," I said. "I'd love to visit the Art Institute again. When do we leave?"

Mom and Dad exchanged looks. "*We,*" Mom stressed the word, pointing her finger at Dad, then at herself, "need to leave on Thursday."

Ohh. This was just a Mom-and-Dad trip, I thought, disappointed.

"We talked to Russ and Peaches," Dad began.

Russ and Peaches are my favorite aunt and uncle, the parents of my favorite cousin, baby Lynn. Having Lynn around all weekend would definitely help make up for missing out on a trip to Chicago.

"But they really have their hands full taking care of Lynn," he finished.

"We can help them with Lynn," I said.

"We have another idea," Mom said. "How would you girls feel about staying here alone? Not alone, exactly, since there would be two of you." She laughed nervously. "We'll only be gone from Thursday evening through Sunday afternoon."

A weekend with no parents? Janine and me here alone, together? I could leave my homework until Sunday night because no one except my sister would be here to help me — and surely she'd have things to do on a weekend with no parents. This was sounding better and better.

I glanced at Janine and found her looking at me, her eyes gleaming in a way I wasn't too sure I liked. She turned to Mom and Dad. "That sounds like a well-thought-out plan to me. I'd be delighted to take care of Claudia."

Take care of? Mom and Dad didn't say anything about Janine "taking care of" me. They said leave us here alone together.

"Claudia?" Everyone's eyes were on me.

"Sounds like a plan to me too. But . . ."

"Wonderful." Mom stood up and actually clapped her hands.

"Of course we'll leave money for pizza one evening," Dad assured us.

"And I'll prepare casseroles and leave them in the freezer," Mom said.

"Claudia and I are perfectly capable of cooking for ourselves. It will be fun, won't it, Claud? Planning meals, cooking them? We can rent a couple of videos. Maybe we can go shopping! I can't wait!"

Again, everyone was staring at me. I forced a smile. The look in Janine's eyes made me wonder what she planned to shop for. Matching sister outfits, maybe?

Already, I was nervous.

CHAPTER 4

Saturday

I sometimes wonder what it would be like to have a brother — whether we'd play soccer all the time. Maybe we'd even play on the same team. But if Melody and Bill Korman are any example, wrestling is the sport of choice for brother and sister.

Abby had known things weren't going very well between Melody and Bill as early as the telephone call she made on Friday, to tell Mrs. Korman she would sit for the kids on Saturday afternoon. She'd hoped that they'd reach a truce before it was time for the sitting job. At first, it seemed as if they had.

Since the Kormans live on Abby's street, she walked to their house.

The doorbell hadn't finished chiming before Mrs. Korman flung open the front door. "Come on in, Abby. We'll be ready in a moment," she said, leading the way to the back of the house.

When they reached the kitchen, Mrs. Korman lifted Skylar out of her high chair and gave her a kiss on the cheek. "Mr. Korman and I are taking Skylar to a gym class this afternoon. We shouldn't be gone too long."

Through the door to the den Abby could see Mr. Korman down on one knee talking to Bill. Bill's arms were folded tightly against his chest and he was looking at the floor.

"The phone number of the gym is posted by the telephone. Melody is upstairs in her room. I'll let her know you're here. I have to grab Skylar's bag," said Mrs. Korman, her eyes darting back and forth between Abby and the scene in the den.

"I'll take Skylar for you." Abby held out her

arms and Skylar buried her head in her mother's shoulder.

Mrs. Korman handed her to Abby.

"Hey, Skylar, are you going to learn to do some somersaults? Cartwheels, maybe?" Abby asked.

Skylar yawned.

"Let's clean you up a little. Everyone will know you had applesauce for lunch." Abby carried her to the sink, ran warm water over a paper towel, and wiped Skylar's face. Skylar twisted her head and pulled away.

"You look all fresh and rosy now. We'll do the same thing to your high chair." Abby picked up the empty bowl with traces of applesauce on the sides and placed it on the counter, then ran the towel over the tray of the high chair.

Mr. Korman joined them and Skylar reached out to him. He took her from Abby. "Did Mrs. Korman tell you where we're going?" he asked.

"Yes. And she showed me the number by the phone."

Mrs. Korman reappeared. "Melody will be down as soon as she finishes picking up the game she and Bill were playing," she said. "What's the weather like? Do we need jackets?"

"It's perfect outside," Abby said.

36

"Let's go." Mrs. Korman held the door for her husband. "Are they going to behave?" Abby heard her say to Mr. Korman as the door shut.

"Hi, Bill!" Abby joined him in the den, where he was slumped on the sofa watching a movie. "How's school?" Bill is nine. He and Melody go to Stoneybrook Day School.

"Okay, I guess. Better than home. At least it keeps me away from my bratty sister for awhile," he said.

"Is this a video?" Abby asked, recognizing the movie.

"Nope. It's on cable today. I love this part," he said, staring at the screen. Abby got the message. He didn't want to be disturbed.

She decided to go upstairs and say hi to Melody, who is seven. As Abby walked to the back staircase, she wondered what it would be like to live in a house this big. Her house is large and so is Kristy's, but the Kormans' house is the biggest one on the street.

Melody was sitting in the middle of the floor, picking up the pieces of a board game, one at a time. "I don't see why Bill doesn't have to help. He was playing too," she said to Abby before Abby had a chance to say a word.

"I think Bill is watching a movie," Abby said. As soon as she saw the expression on Melody's face, she wished she hadn't mentioned it.

Melody jumped to her feet. "He knew I wanted to watch the cartoon marathon. And Mom said I could." She pushed past Abby and ran downstairs.

Abby followed close behind.

"It's my turn to watch the television in here," Melody announced as she barged into the den. She picked up the remote control and switched the channel. "Mom said I could at lunch, and I know you heard her."

"Did you hear your mom say that, Bill?" Abby asked.

"Let her watch her cartoons. I'll go upstairs and watch in Mom and Dad's bedroom."

"Fine. I don't want you in here anyway." Melody curled up on the couch.

"That's a good idea. Thanks, Bill, for being so cooperative." Abby smiled at him and reached out to give him a high five as he walked past, but he ignored her.

"How about a snack? I could fix something," Abby suggested, hoping to improve their moods a little. "What sounds good?"

"There's ice cream and chocolate syrup and whipped cream in a can," Melody said. "You could make sundaes."

"Sounds good to me. Bill?" He had stopped at the bottom of the staircase when Abby mentioned the snack.

"Okay. Will you bring it up when it's ready?

I don't want to miss any more of the movie."

Abby thought a moment. She didn't like setting a precedent of waiting on kids, but he had agreed to go upstairs pretty easily. "Sure. It'll take a few minutes."

Bill disappeared up the staircase.

In the freezer, Abby found vanilla ice cream. She set it out on the counter while she gathered the rest of the ingredients. There was a jar of cherries in the pantry, so she decided to add a cherry to each sundae.

The ice cream was hard packed and she had to let it soften for awhile. Just as she decided it was ready to scoop, Bill stomped through the kitchen.

"Bill! What's going on?" she called after him. There was no answer.

Abby filled the bowls with ice cream, poured on chocolate syrup, covered it all with whipped cream, then dropped a cherry on top of each sundae. As she was placing the bowls on a tray to take into the den, she heard a shriek.

Hoping that the sight of her ice-cream creation would end whatever problem was brewing, Abby picked up the tray and rushed into the room. Melody was standing in front of the television screen, blocking the picture.

"Out of the way, I said. I'm missing my movie," Bill yelled.

"I thought you were going to watch it up-stairs," Abby said.

"That TV is too little. I can't see a thing. She can watch her dumb cartoons up there. Who cares whether you can see them or not? Melody, move out of the way right now."

"No! I'm watching what I want." She leaned against the screen.

Bill ran to her and gave a her a shove out of the way, then grabbed the remote control. Melody held on tightly to it.

"Stop! Stop it right now," Abby said firmly, looking for a safe place to set the tray.

Melody and Bill fell to the floor, wrestling for control of the remote. Bill stood up, pointing the device toward the TV and changing the channel. Abby parked the ice cream on a table far away from the wrestling match and moved in toward Bill and Melody.

Before Abby could reach them, Melody grabbed Bill's arm. Bill shoved her, harder this time, and his sister fell back, hitting her head on the sofa with a *thunk*. She screamed.

Abby dropped to her knees beside Melody. "Are you okay?" she asked.

"My head! I hit my head!" Melody wailed. "It was his fault. He pushed me. You saw him!" Her cries rose and fell as Abby checked for blood or a bump and didn't feel anything seri-ous.

"Shh!" Abby pulled her close and rocked Melody back and forth. "There's no blood. We'll put some ice on your head and it will be fine."

Bill backed toward the door. "Wait a minute," Abby said to him. "Melody, you sit here on the sofa while I find an ice bag."

Melody nodded and wiped her face. "What about my ice cream?" she asked.

Abby shook her head. "It's a shame you were hurt and Bill shouldn't have pushed you. But you were fighting too."

Bill was reaching for one of the bowls of ice cream.

Abby picked up the remote control and turned off the television. "Bill, please put that down and tell Melody you're sorry."

"I am *not* sorry," he said and shoved a spoonful of sundae into his mouth.

Melody started to whimper again.

"You need to go to your room and think about why you're not ready to apologize to your sister," Abby suggested.

Bill slammed his bowl onto the table and stomped out of the room.

Taking a deep breath, Abby picked up the tray of sundaes. Ice cream wasn't an option in the present climate.

In the kitchen, Abby dumped the melted sundaes into the garbage disposal, then grabbed a bag of frozen peas out of the freezer. It would make a perfect ice bag.

"Can I watch my show now?" Melody asked Abby as she entered the den.

"I think we'll leave the television off for awhile," Abby said. "Where did you hit your head?"

"Here." Melody pointed to the back of her head.

Abby draped the "ice bag" over the injured spot. "Does the ice help any?" she asked.

Melody nodded and the bag slipped off. Abby rearranged it. "You need to sit quietly or it won't stay in place," she said. She spotted a copy of *Ramona Quimby, Age 8* on the end table. "Would you like me to read to you while you rest?" Abby asked.

Melody nodded again and the bag slipped again. "You might want to hold it in place," Abby suggested. She opened the book and started reading.

They were starting the third chapter when Abby heard the garage door open.

"It's Mom and Dad." Melody jumped up. Still holding the peas in place she ran to the back door.

"What happened to you, young lady?" Mrs. Korman said.

Melody sniffed once and then burst into tears. Mrs. Korman gathered her up in a hug and looked at Abby. Then Mr. Korman entered, carrying a sleeping Skylar, and headed up the stairs, looking briefly at his wife and older daughter and frowning.

"Bill, he . . . he grabbed the remote control and he threw me down on the ground and jumped on top of me, hitting me and hitting me until I couldn't hold on to it anymore. Then I tried to take it back and he pushed me real hard and I fell into the couch and hit my head. And it really hurts." Melody cried into her mother's shirt.

Mrs. Korman looked at Abby again.

"Bill and Melody were arguing over the remote control. He did push her, and she fell, but . . ." Abby began, wanting to explain that both the children had been fighting.

"Not again," said Mrs. Korman in a tired voice. She wriggled free of Melody. "What started the argument over the remote?"

"You said I could watch cartoons, but Bill was watching a movie."

"We have two televisions in this house," said Mrs. Korman.

"But Bill didn't want to watch upstairs and neither did I," Melody explained. "When he changed the channel, I stood in front of the TV and that's when he started pushing me."

Mrs. Korman sighed.

Mr. Korman and Bill came downstairs.

"What's this all about?" Mr. Korman asked. "Melody, Bill says that you wouldn't let him watch television with you."

"They both wanted to watch the television in the den, but they wanted to watch different shows," Abby explained. "While I was fixing a snack, they started arguing over the remote and things got a little rough. Bill shoved Melody and she hit her head."

"People may get hurt when you use your hands instead of words to work things out," Mrs. Korman said to Bill. "I think you owe your sister an apology for pushing her so hard."

"But it wasn't my fault," said Bill. "She was standing in front of the TV and nobody else could see it."

"Bill," Mr. Korman said, a note of warning in his voice.

"No. I'm not sorry. She's a big tattletale baby." Bill folded his arms across his chest.

"You'll go to your room right now, young man. And you may consider yourself grounded," Mr. Korman announced as Bill stomped away once again.

"I'm really sorry that this happened, Mrs. Korman," said Abby. "I think Melody's okay. There's only a small bump and the skin wasn't broken." In fact, Melody was wearing a half smile as she watched her brother disappear.

"It's not your fault, Abby. This is becoming all too common in our house these days." Mrs. Korman tucked her hair behind her ears. "Melody, go into the den and turn on your cartoons for awhile. Bill won't bother you again."

Melody's smile grew and she skipped into the den.

"I'm going to go see Bill before I leave, if that's okay," Abby said. She knew how hard it was to admit being wrong, but maybe she could talk to him and make him see that he should apologize to Melody.

"Sure, go ahead." Mrs Korman picked up the bag of peas Melody had dropped on the floor. Mr. Korman filled a teakettle with water and set it on the stove.

Upstairs, Abby knocked softly on the door to Bill's room.

"Who is it?" he asked.

"Abby. I came to say good-bye. May I come in?"

"Good-bye," Bill said grumpily.

Abby opened the door partway but didn't step inside. "I know how easy it is to say something hurtful or do something you'll regret later. But I always feel better once I apologize."

"I don't," Bill insisted. "The brat deserved it."

Abby backed away. Bill had his mind made up.

The door to Bill's room slammed behind her. And Abby headed for home.

CHAPTER 5

I'm not a morning person, especially on weekends. I like to stay in bed and think in pictures. I close my eyes and see paintings I'd like to make, sculptures I'd like to create, scenes I'd like to photograph. I also think about clothes. That's what I was doing when the phone rang early (early for me, not for the rest of the world) on Saturday morning.

"Hello," I mumbled. It was the first word I'd spoken that day, and I can understand why someone would think I was still asleep.

"Claudia? Is this Claudia?" Josh asked, sounding unsure.

I sat up. "Hi, Josh. It's me."

"Are you okay?"

"Yeah, are you?"

"When you didn't call last night, I started to worry. And then when you answered the phone . . ."

I pulled my knees up and rested my forehead against them. I'd forgotten to call Josh, after I'd promised I would.

"Claudia? Are you there? Knock, knock," he said.

"I'm here and I'm fine. Except I feel awful about not calling you last night. Janine helped me with my math homework, then my mom and dad came in with this big announcement, then they surprised us with a video. Josh, I'm really, truly sorry I forgot." And I was.

"That's okay. As long as you're all right."

That was Josh through and through. He was worried about me instead of being angry.

"What are you doing now?" he asked.

"Thinking about what I'm going to wear tonight. You can still go, can't you?" All of a sudden, I started to worry that he was calling me with bad news.

"I remember — you, me, Mary Anne, Logan, Stacey, and some extra cool guy from the city. In fact, I was calling to remind you. In case you'd forgotten that too."

It was a dig, but it was a gentle one, and I deserved it.

"Where are we going?" Josh asked.

"Dinner at the Rosebud Cafe, then maybe a video at Stacey's. We're meeting everyone around six at the Rosebud."

"Claud, what should I wear? I mean, what will the other guys be wearing?"

I detected something new in Josh's voice. Was he nervous? Surely not. He knew Stacey and Mary Anne, even Logan. "It's just dinner and a video. No big deal," I assured him.

"But what will I say to all those people?"

He *was* nervous. "Josh, I've never known you to run out of things to say. And it's not really 'all those people.' You know everybody except Ethan. It'll be fun."

"Sure," Josh said. Then he added, "Is there any chance there'll be a few hours in the day when we're not with your friends or getting ready to be with your friends?"

My friends? I was starting to feel like taffy being pulled in too many directions by too many people — Josh, my other seventh-grade friends, and my friends in the BSC. "I know Mom and Dad are going to make me do some more homework. But why don't you come over a little early? Dad will drive us to the Rosebud when it's time," I suggested.

I could almost hear his smile when he agreed. "I'll be there. You can coach me on how to act with cool older guys."

I giggled. "I'm such an expert! See you later." We hung up and I dragged my body out of bed.

"You're looking pretty good," Josh said when I answered his knock later that day.

"Only pretty good?" I pretended to be insulted. I'd worked hard on my outfit — a long black skirt, a white shirt with full sleeves, and a short vest that I'd covered with bright-colored buttons and bows. My hair was braided with strands of ribbons that matched the decorations on the vest.

Then I looked at Josh. How could I tell him that maybe he'd overdressed a bit? I didn't know if I'd ever seen anybody in the Rosebud Cafe wearing a tie, unless it was somebody's dad. Josh also had on a denim shirt and khaki pants. The outfit wouldn't be bad at all if he lost the tie.

"You didn't have to dress up for me!" I teased, pulling on the tie.

Josh stepped back and adjusted the knot. "You'll strangle me if you keep pulling on it like that."

"Come on in." I stood aside, then shut the door after him.

"Hi, Josh," my mom called, sticking her head around the corner.

"Hi, Mrs. Kishi. Thanks for letting me come over," he said.

"Our pleasure."

Janine was watching television in the den. "We'll go someplace else," I said, backing out.

Too late. Janine stood up, causing the remote

control to fly into the air. It landed at Josh's feet.

"Your electronic wand, milady," he said, handing it back to her with a bow.

Janine laughed — a little too loudly, I thought. "Thank you, gallant sir," she answered. "You're more than welcome to join me. I was channel swimming, trying to find something fit to watch."

"I think you mean channel *surfing*, Janine," I corrected her.

Josh plopped down on the sofa. When I sat down beside him, he rested his arm along the back, barely touching my shoulders. "You have some big plans tonight?" he asked Janine.

"I might bake some cookies," she replied. We hadn't gotten around to it the night before. "Any special kind you guys like?"

"Anything with chocolate in it," I said.

"Maybe when you're through with dinner, we could make some chocolate-chip cookies."

Two nights in a row with nothing to do but hang out and bake cookies? That seemed odd even for Janine. "We're going to Stacey's after dinner," I reminded her. I thought I felt Josh's arm stiffen when I mentioned going to Stacey's, but he was smiling when I glanced at him.

"Janine, could you help me for a minute in the kitchen?" Mom called.

Thank you, Mom, I thought.

Josh and I settled back on the couch as Janine left, promising to come back as soon as she'd finished helping Mom.

"What did you do today?" I asked him, leaning back against his arm.

"Rescued my cat from a fate worse than death."

"Is he okay?" I asked.

"Only his pride is wounded. There's another cat in the neighborhood. We call it the 'puffy' cat because it has hair out to here." Josh held his hands wide apart. "It hangs around our house all the time, waiting for my cat to come outside. I've never been sure whether it wants to play with him or fight him. Then today I decided it wasn't waiting for my cat at all. It was waiting for us. I think it's jealous of all the attention we give our cat."

"How did you figure that out?" I asked.

"Because all it wants is to be petted. As soon as any one of us steps outside, it starts meowing and rubbing against our legs. Except for Dad. Dad's yelled at it before and it doesn't like him much. In fact, one of the neighbors asked why Dad was so mean to the poor cat. He's not mean. He's just trying to make it go away and leave our cat alone."

I laughed, imagining Mr. Rocker chasing the "puffy" cat away.

"You guys ready to go?" Dad asked from the doorway.

Josh whirled around, then smoothed his hair and straightened his tie again.

When he reached the car, Josh held the back door open for me, then climbed in beside me. He was quiet on the way to the restaurant, answering Dad's questions but not saying much else.

"Thanks for the ride, Mr. Kishi," Josh said as we climbed out of the car. His voice broke slightly when he said "Kishi," but he quickly cleared his throat to cover it.

"See you later, Dad. Mrs. McGill will drive us home later," I said.

"Have a good evening." Dad waved as we turned to walk inside.

Josh paused at the door. I grabbed his hand and found it damp with sweat. He pulled it away and dried it on his pants. "Still want to hold it?" he asked with a grin, rubbing it on his pants leg again.

I took his hand and smiled, trying to reassure him.

We were the last ones to arrive.

"Welcome to the Rosebud Cafe," Logan said, standing up and bowing as we approached the table.

"Claudia!" Stacey looked surprised to see us. She'd been deep in conversation with Ethan, who was every bit as cute as I'd remembered. He was dressed all in black — black jeans and a black long-sleeved shirt. "And Josh," she added.

There were two empty chairs between Ethan and Mary Anne, so I took the one near Ethan, leaving Josh to sit beside Mary Anne. He knew her, and maybe that would help him feel more relaxed. He kept wiping his hands on his pants and clearing his throat.

"Claudia, you remember Ethan. Ethan, this is Josh Rocker, who goes to school with us. Josh, this is my friend Ethan Carroll, from New York City." I was glad that Stacey didn't mention that Josh was in seventh grade. That was one of the things making him nervous.

Josh had just sat down, but he quickly pushed his chair back and stood to shake Ethan's hand. His chair tipped over when he stood up, making a huge racket. Worse, a waiter was passing behind him when the chair fell. He stopped short, and the tray he was carrying tilted. The glasses on the tray began to slide. Josh grabbed the tray and leveled it, let go, and jumped back, landing in Mary Anne's lap.

"Are you all right?" the waiter asked Josh.

"Fine," Josh said. "Hi, Mary Anne. Sure is good to see you again."

Everyone laughed.

"It's nice to meet you, Josh," said Ethan.

"You too, earring — I mean, Ethan." Josh's face turned red again.

Ethan has one ear pierced. I guess it caught Josh's attention.

We relaxed. Josh began talking to Logan. I turned to Ethan and asked him if he'd been to any good art exhibits lately. He is a terrific artist. We were discussing an exhibition of collages he'd seen recently when Josh nudged me.

"I'll be right back," he whispered. He headed to the men's room. When he returned, his tie was gone.

When our food arrived, Josh concentrated on his dinner, nodding or shaking his head and chewing whenever someone asked him a question. He looked more relaxed by the time we'd finished eating and arrived at Stacey's house.

During the video, Josh and Logan talked quietly about sports for awhile. Then Josh leaned his head back against the couch and closed his eyes for a few minutes. The movie *was* pretty boring. I wondered if Ethan had chosen it, because it didn't seem like something Stacey would ordinarily watch. It had subtitles and beautiful scenery but not much happening. I wasn't even sure what it was about.

"I guess all the copies of *Mask of the Avenger* were already rented," Josh whispered to me toward the end of the movie.

After the video, Mr. Spier showed up to drive us home. I'd thought that Mrs. McGill was going to do that, but it didn't matter. Dad wouldn't mind if I rode with Mary Anne's dad. We dropped Josh off first.

"I'll call you tomorrow," he said. "Thanks for the ride, Mr. Spier. Good night." Josh almost didn't wait for the car to come to a complete stop before he jumped out and ran up the walk to the door of his house.

"Do you think Josh had a good time?" Mary Anne asked. "He's really sweet."

"And funny," Logan added.

"Yeah, I think it went pretty well," I said, feeling pleasantly tired.

When we reached my house, all the lights were on. Janine was standing in the hall, holding a plate of cookies. "Isn't anybody else coming in?" she asked, looking past me to the door.

"It's kind of late," I said.

"Oh." Janine looked down at the cookies.

"I'll have a couple," I said. They were chocolate chip — I think. The edges were too dark and the shapes were all a little different. I bit into one and it crunched.

"They're a little overdone," Janine said. "I was reading and didn't hear the buzzer. How was your date?" She turned and carried the cookies back into the kitchen.

"Fun," I said, starting upstairs.

"Aren't you going to tell me about it?"

"Sure." I joined my sister in the kitchen. Janine was beginning to act like my new best friend. I was just thinking that her bonding attempts probably wouldn't go on much longer when Janine pulled out . . . the list.

"I brainstormed a selection of activities for next weekend when Mom and Dad are gone. What do you think?" Janine asked.

The list covered the front and half of the back of a piece of paper. I thought that if we did even half of the things she'd written down I'd never have time for Josh, the BSC, my seventh-grade friends, and my homework.

CHAPTER 6

"Thanks for the cookies, Janine," Josh called over his shoulder as we headed down the sidewalk. It was the next day, and we still had *plenty* of Janine's cookies left.

"Anytime. I'm hopeful they'll prove to be a delight to the palate," my sister replied.

We were on our way to eat pizza. I'd just finished my homework, when Josh had called. As soon as I'd said yes to pizza and hung up the phone, Stacey called to talk about Ethan. Like I said — taffy pull time.

As we walked into Pizza Express, a couple of Josh's friends called to us from the video game arcade. Josh waved to them. Then we chose a table for two along the wall.

"I like this place," Josh said after we ordered.

"Me too." Practically everybody I know likes Pizza Express.

"It's kind of . . . comfortable here," he continued.

I nodded.

"Not like the Rosebud." Josh arranged and rearranged the napkin holder and the cheese and spice containers sitting on the edge of the table.

"The Rosebud isn't so bad," I said.

"But you have to worry about table manners, and talking with your mouth full, and," he shrugged, "not being immature."

"I guess you didn't have much fun last night," I said.

"I don't know if I did or not. I was so nervous. I wore a tie and almost knocked out a waiter with my chair. I didn't have a clue about what to say to anybody."

"I knew you were nervous at first, but I didn't realize it was that bad."

The waitress set our pizza on the table. Josh transferred a large slice from the pan to his plate. Strings of cheese stretched between the pizza and his slice. He stuck his fingers underneath them and twirled, separating the cheese from the rest of the pie. "I couldn't have done that last night, in front of everybody. How old is Ethan anyway?"

"Fifteen," I said.

"He was so . . ." Josh took a bite and chewed, thinking. "He didn't make a single mistake all night."

"Still, he may have been as nervous as you

were but was covering it up. I know I was worried the first time I met him. But he's cool."

"Yeah. I wish I could have gotten through it that easily."

"You did fine."

"I felt better after I ditched the tie," Josh said with a smile. He leaned his head back and let the string of cheese dribble into his mouth.

"You and Logan were talking. I bet Logan felt awkward at first too."

"Is Logan part of the BSC?" Josh asked.

"He's an associate member. He takes jobs if the rest of us are busy," I explained.

"He must get a lot of jobs, then," Josh said.

I sighed. One of the things I like about Josh is that he's easy to talk to. "You mean you think I'm too busy?"

"Not exactly. It's more that you have separate groups of friends. One group goes with this part of your life," Josh tore his pizza slice in half and put one part of it on his plate. "And another group goes with this part." He placed the second half on a napkin. "I'm part of this seventh-grade group, but I don't know the BSC group that well. And, sometimes I'd like to be our own group — Josh and Claudia."

"I feel more like a piece of taffy than pizza," I said. "Pulled and tugged between my friends, my family, and homework. I wish there was a fun way to bring everybody together," I added, thinking out loud. "Like a party."

"How about a taffy pull?"

I laughed. "I was thinking of a get-acquainted party."

"That sounds like fun. Why not do it?" Josh asked.

I shook my head. "I don't think my parents would let me throw a big party."

After Josh walked me home I tried to come up with another way to bring the different groups in my life together. As I passed by Janine's room, she spun her chair toward the door. "Did Josh enjoy the cookies?" she called out.

I wasn't sure what he'd done with the cookies, but I called out, "Yeah," and continued toward my room.

I sat on my bed. I knew my friends would like one another if they had a chance to get to know one another better. I looked up to see Janine in the doorway, leaning against the jamb.

"Did you finish your science assignment?" she asked.

"Mom helped me with it. She wouldn't let me go out with Josh until I finished."

Janine continued to stand there. "Would you like to join me in a game of — "

"I don't think so," I said before she could even finish asking. Janine likes games that test the brain, and I'm no match for her. "Don't you have something to study tonight?"

"I'm reading the most fascinating book for extra credit in my English class. It's a novel about chess. You know I don't usually enjoy fiction, but this particular plot is almost mathematical in its precision," she said.

"Sounds great," I mumbled as I felt underneath the bed for the bag of M&M's I knew was there. When I pulled it out, Janine was holding out her hand. I poured some M&M's into it. Maybe I could get used to spending time with Janine.

"You know," said Janine thoughtfully, "you've managed to maintain relationships with your seventh-grade friends as well as your eighth-grade friends, even now that you've returned to the eighth grade, haven't you?"

"I'm trying," I said, suddenly realizing that my problem wasn't so bad after all. Here I was, feeling as if I had too many friends, but it seemed as if Janine didn't have any friends at all. Maybe that's why she was so interested in my life all of a sudden.

"We could work ahead in your math book," Janine suggested.

"Nah," I said.

"Maybe I'll go back to my room." She popped the last two M&M's into her mouth. "See you in the morning."

"See you," I said, collapsing back against the pillows. How could I fit more hours into the day? That's the only solution I could come up with for managing to keep all my friends happy.

By the time our Monday BSC meeting rolled around, I still hadn't come up with any ideas about how to bring my seventh-grade friends, Josh, and my BSC friends together.

Abby had run to the meeting again, and Jessi was showing her some stretches that she could do to cool down. Stacey was writing in the BSC notebook, and Mary Anne and Kristy were looking at a magazine. Mallory was sitting on the floor, leaning against my bed. She seemed to be studying her fingernails.

"How did you do on your social studies test?" Stacey asked Mal as she handed her the BSC notebook.

"Okay. I think I got an eighty-six." Mal passed the notebook to Mary Anne without even opening it. She had barely smiled when she'd arrived that afternoon and hadn't smiled once since. And an 86 on a test? Usually, she'd consider that near failing. I noticed Jessi's look of concern when Mal announced her grade. We were all concerned about Mal.

"Did Josh have a good time Saturday night?" Mary Anne asked.

"He said he was too nervous to enjoy it," I admitted.

Mary Anne nodded. "Logan said the same thing."

"Ethan thought everything went pretty well, considering. He said meeting new people isn't his favorite thing," said Stacey.

So I'd been right. All the guys had felt as awkward as Josh had. "But sometimes it's good to mix with different people," I said.

"When?" asked Mary Anne.

"When you've just beaten the pants off them at softball," Kristy said.

"When you're trying out for a part in a ballet," Jessi offered.

"When you're running past them on the street," mumbled Abby, her head touching the floor between her outstretched legs. I stared in wonder. I knew I couldn't do that.

"I don't know which is worse: meeting new people who don't know anything about you, or having to see the same old faces and hear the same old comments every single day," Mallory said.

Her response was the only one that was serious.

"What I mean is that I had to meet new people and make new friends when I went back to seventh grade, and those people are still my friends," I said.

"Yeah?" said Stacey.

"And I wish there was some way they could get to know you guys and you guys could get to know them."

"What if we went out for pizza together?" Abby suggested.

I figured Josh wouldn't be very anxious to go out to eat with a new group of people anytime soon.

"We could go to the mall together," Stacey said.

"Josh may have had one too many shopping trips with 'the girls' already," I answered.

"Well, you'll come up with something," Stacey assured me.

I wished I could feel as confident about that as Stacey sounded. I wondered how hard taffy had to be pulled before it broke apart.

CHAPTER 7

*W*hat *a day to be late*, I thought as I ran the last block home on Thursday afternoon. Mom and Dad had a plane to catch and I'd left school only after promising to call Joanna, then Stacey, and finally Josh. With Mom and Dad gone, I might be able to do it.

The front door hit a suitcase when I opened it. "I'm here!" I called out as soon as I'd caught my breath enough to speak.

"About time!" Mom said as she and Dad joined me in the hall. "We were worried the car would arrive before you did. Janine, we're almost ready. Come on down."

Mom opened the door and looked outside. "Oh, the car is here now. We did almost miss you." She hugged me.

"I left the phone number of the hotel along with that of the Simpsons posted beside the phone in the kitchen," Dad said as he slipped on his overcoat.

"If anyone calls, take a message and tell them we'll call back. For heaven's sake, don't tell them we're gone for the weekend," Mom reminded us. This was something I'd known to do since kindergarten.

"Check to make sure the doors are locked before you go to bed," Dad added.

"Mom. Dad. I'm perfectly capable of remembering the basic rules of safety at home," Janine said. I nodded.

"Don't hesitate to call Russ and Peaches if you need anything, anything at all," Mom said. "Claudia, your face is flushed. You don't feel feverish, do you?"

"I was hurrying home to tell you good-bye. I feel fine." I took her hand and placed it on my forehead so she could feel for herself.

"If you do feel ill . . ."

"I'll call the pediatrician, Russ and Peaches, the Simpsons, the neighbors, and put an ad in the paper," Janine said. Then she picked up Mom's suitcase and handed it to her.

"You go and have a good time. We'll be fine," I said. I kissed Dad, then Mom.

"There are casseroles in the freezer. The instructions for heating them are on the containers." Mom had stopped halfway down the walk to turn around and tell us about the food.

"I know," Janine said, "and there's cash

available for any additional groceries we might need."

"Quiet about the cash," Mom said, placing her finger over her lips.

I hoped that pizza qualified as a grocery we might need.

"I have everything under control," Janine called out as Mom and Dad climbed into the car.

We waved until the car pulled away from the curb, then went inside. Janine closed the door and locked it.

"No parents for three days," she said, her eyes shining. "It's you and me, Claudia. Shall we consult our list of activities? There's a great special on the Discovery Channel tonight about the *Titanic*."

I was looking forward to the weekend too, but I wasn't planning to spend all my time with my sister. "You know, even though they're gone, I know Mom and Dad would want me to keep up with my homework. I think I'll go upstairs and start — "

"Of course. I wouldn't dream of interfering with your study time," Janine said quickly. "I promised I would stand in for Mom and Dad as your homework mentor."

"Thanks, Janine. When I'm finished, I'll let you check it." I started up the steps to my room.

"We could rent a movie. Have you seen *Sense and Sensibility*? It's a superb adaptation of the Jane Austen novel. It is on the sentimental side, but the literary quality of the story and the language — "

"I don't know, Janine."

"This is the perfect opportunity for us to spend time together. I know! I was exploring the Internet recently and I came upon a wonderful presentation of an art exhibit. You'd love it." Janine looked so eager for me to agree to do something with her.

I figured I could scan the pictures pretty quickly and be on the phone in no time. "Maybe when I'm finished with my homework we can look at it," I said.

"Excellent. There are links to other exhibits of interest that we could explore together."

Another person who wanted a piece of me. The taffy was being pulled thinner and thinner.

"I'll take on the evening meal. I have something in mind already." Janine turned toward the kitchen as I trudged up the stairs.

When I reached my room, I dumped my books on the bed, found a Hershey bar I'd hidden in an old purse in my closet, took a big bite, then made myself sit down at my desk and open my science book. I needed to write up a report of an experiment we'd done in class this week. I'd taken notes and planned to draw a diagram to go along with the answers to the questions assigned. Maybe I'd receive extra credit for the drawing, to make up for what I might lose for misspellings.

Before I could sit down at the desk, the phone rang. It was Peaches.

"Are your parents gone?" she asked.

"They're gone. It's me and Janine." I knew my favorite aunt would understand what I meant.

"What about dinner? Do you know what you're going to have for dinner?" she asked.

"Janine has it under control."

"Maybe I should talk to Janine."

"She's in the kitchen. Maybe you could call her on the other phone," I suggested. "I'm doing homework."

"Homework. Absolutely. Your mother mentioned that you were to keep up with your homework. I'll let you go. Call me if you need anything."

" 'Bye, Peaches." I hung up.

The family phone rang about half a dozen times as I finished my science homework and started my math, but Janine never said anything, so I supposed the calls were for her.

I was working on my last math problem when Janine called me to dinner.

After I washed my hands, I headed to the kitchen. But Janine was in the dining room.

The table was set with Mom's good china and silver and there were candles burning — along with the overhead light.

"Everything looks awfully nice," I said.

"I thought our first night on our own was cause for celebration," Janine explained. "Spaghetti?"

"I love spaghetti!"

"The sauce is something new — garlic, olive oil, fresh tomatoes, and a variety of spices. I hope you enjoy it."

"It's good," I said in between bites.

"You should eat some of the salad also." Janine pushed a bowl toward me.

"Thanks. Great meal." I meant it. Spaghetti is one of my absolute favorite foods in the whole world. "Who called so many times?"

"Peaches, then Russ, then Russ again, then Peaches again. I was almost glad when the last call was someone trying to sell us a long-distance service."

"What did Russ and Peaches want?" I asked.

"To know if we knew the number at the hotel, what I was fixing for dinner, and whether we needed anything from the store." She shrugged, then said, "I almost forgot the garlic bread." Janine handed me a basket.

"With all the work you did on the meal, you must have a ton of homework to do after dinner," I said hopefully.

"I finished most of it in study hall, then completed the remainder while the food was cooking," Janine said. "It won't interfere with our time." She was determined that we spend the evening together. "Save room for dessert," she added as I reached for more spaghetti. "Vanilla ice cream with caramel sauce served with blondies."

"Are you sure there isn't someone else in the kitchen?" I turned around and pretended to search.

Janine had finished her meal, so I ate a few more bites of salad, then pushed my chair back. "I'll do the dishes since you fixed the meal." I stacked the plates, then the bowls.

"Finish your homework. I'll load the dishwasher, then navigate to the virtual art exhibit I was telling you about. By then you should be ready." Janine nodded her head in the direction of the steps.

"That sounds great," I said with as much enthusiasm as I could muster.

I only had a little bit of English left once I'd finished my math. I still had hopes that I'd find time to call Josh and Stacey, after Janine and I bonded a little.

My phone rang. I reached for the receiver, expecting Peaches. It was Joanna. She had a question about her social studies homework for me, Claudia Kishi. I like being the source of information for a change rather than the one who needs help.

"Who's on the phone?" Janine was at the door to my room.

I covered the mouth of the receiver. "Joanna."

"Tell her hi. And I called up that Web site." Janine backed away.

"I have to go. My sister wants to show me something on the computer. Talk to you tomorrow."

"This is a partial showing of works collected by Catherine the Great, the Russian empress." Janine pointed to the oil painting reproduced on her computer screen, when I joined her a few minutes later.

"How do you get to the next screen?" I asked. In spite of myself, I wanted to see what else Catherine had owned.

Janine clicked the mouse and the picture changed to a hunt scene. The colors showed up very well on the computer screen. I reached for the mouse and clicked. The screen went blank. "What happened?"

"Let me see." Janine took control of the mouse again. While she was absorbed in finding the way back to the artwork, I decided to call Stacey.

"My parents will be back on Sunday afternoon," I was saying when Janine appeared at the door again.

"Who is it this time?" she asked.

"Stacey."

"Hi, Stacey! Tell her that I found a wonderful fashion Web site."

"Janine found something about fashion on the Internet she thinks you'd like." I relayed Stacey's response to Janine. "She said maybe she can look at it when she comes to the next BSC meeting."

"I found it rather by accident," Janine confessed, "but I thought of Stacey immediately."

I smiled and nodded, trying to listen to Janine and Stacey at the same time.

"I recovered the display," Janine went on.

"I'll be there in a minute. Stacey, I have to go. Maybe I can call you back a little later. I want to know what was in the letter from Ethan. See you!"

"Now the screen is frozen," Janine said when I finally rejoined her in her room.

"I'm going to call Josh while you're working on it." I hurried back to my room and punched in his number. He answered so quickly that I thought he must have been waiting by the phone.

"How's your first night without parents going?" he asked.

"The without-parents part is good, but the with-sister bit is a little odd. Janine wants us to do stuff together. You should see the look in her eyes when she talks about it. I feel as if I'm some new math problem she's determined to solve."

"Did you have much homework? Joanna called to ask me about the social studies assignment."

"Too simple," Josh said.

"Is that Josh?" Janine was back.

I nodded.

"Give him my regards."

I repeated the message.

"Regards back to her," Josh said.

I repeated that. There I was in the middle again. Maybe I could act as a central switchboard. All my friends could call in, and I'd pass messages back and forth between them. That would let them know one another better. It wouldn't be as good as a party, but . . .

"Josh, I have to go. Janine and I have something to discuss. Talk to you tomorrow." I hung up.

"What do we have to talk about?" Janine asked.

Something incredible had just occurred to me. And this weekend would be the perfect time for it. Mom and Dad hadn't said anything about not having friends over. Now if I could just convince Janine.

"Now that I've moved back to eighth grade, I don't have much time to spend with Joanna, Jeannie, Shira, and Josh," I began.

"I'm sure that's a problem," said Janine.

"And my BSC friends haven't had a real chance to mix with my seventh-grade friends," I continued.

Janine nodded.

"Mom and Dad didn't say anything about not having friends over, so I was thinking about inviting everybody here for awhile on Saturday night?" I made it sound like a question and crossed my fingers that Janine would say it was okay.

"Mom and Dad are certainly well acquainted with all of the BSC members. They don't know the seventh-grade contingent quite as well, although they've seemed pleased with your new friends," Janine said, staring at a spot above my head. "I don't see any harm in a simple gathering."

Yes! I was going to have my party.

CHAPTER 8

Friday

I have had to deal with two older brothers my entire life. Melody Korman has only one, and she is having a harder time with him than I've ever had with my two. I can't quite put my finger on what's the matter between them. Bill keeps picking on her, digging himself deeper into trouble every time. But Melody isn't very nice to Bill either. I don't think I was much help....

After spending the afternoon baby-sitting for the two older Kormans, Dr. Kristy still couldn't come up with a diagnosis for their problems. She said that after only two hours, she felt as if she'd been there for two days. Even Mrs. Korman seemed to be discouraged.

"No matter what Bill tells you, he is still grounded," Mrs. Korman said to Kristy as she bundled Skylar into a jacket and prepared to leave.

It had been almost a week since the pushing incident. Kristy was surprised that Bill was still grounded. Her surprise must have shown on her face, because Mrs. Korman went on to explain, "Last Saturday was the worst incident, but he seems to be unable to say one positive word to his sister."

"Sometimes he has to stay in his room the whole evening," Melody said.

"Skylar and I will be gone for an hour or so," Mrs. Korman said, opening the door to the garage. "You have my cellular phone number if you need anything."

" 'Bye, Skylar. 'Bye, Mom." Melody gave each of them a kiss.

Kristy looked up the stairs as the door closed. "Maybe I should say hi to Bill."

Melody shrugged. "He's not going to say

anything to you. And if he does, it will be mean."

After listening to the reports about Bill's behavior from Mrs. Korman and Melody, Kristy wished she didn't have to go upstairs, but she knew she should at least tell Bill she was there if he needed anything.

Melody followed her up the stairs but hung back when Kristy knocked on Bill's door.

"What do you want?" he asked, flinging open the door.

"Hi to you too, Bill," Kristy said.

"Hi, Kristy," he answered in a slightly nicer tone. "The brat isn't with you, is she?"

"If you're talking about Melody, no. But we did want to know if you wanted to come downstairs and play Yahtzee. In fact, I challenge you. I need to make up for the last time you beat me."

"Yahtzee? You and me?" Bill asked, his frown disappearing.

"And Melody," Kristy added.

Bill's expression grew sullen again. "If I have to play with her, then can David Michael and Karen come over?"

"You're grounded," Kristy reminded him.

"But that only means I can't go anyplace."

"I don't think so. Your mother said you were grounded, and she didn't say you could have friends over."

Bill's eyebrows formed a single line above his eyes.

"Then may *I* invite David Michael and Karen over?" Melody asked from behind Kristy.

"David Michael and Karen won't want to come over if they have to be in the same room with doggy breath," Bill said. He started to close his door, but Kristy moved her foot so he couldn't.

"They will too. They like me as much as they like you," Melody cried, tears welling in her eyes.

"Call them and see," Bill said.

"No one is calling David Michael or Karen or anyone else to invite them over here. You're *grounded*, Bill," Kristy said firmly. "Melody is trying to be nice and figure out a way to go around the rules, but it isn't going to work."

"If David Michael was here, we could play in my room, and Karen and bug eyes could play in her room. I wouldn't be talking to her at all," Bill pointed out. "In fact, I promise not to say one bad thing if David Michael comes over."

Kristy shook her head. "That's not the way it works. You show me you can be decent to Melody, then you'll be able to have friends over again. You can start right now by telling her you're sorry for the things you've said just now."

Bill stuck out his tongue at his sister. "You

ruin everything," he yelled, and closed his door.

Kristy removed her foot just in time to avoid having it crushed by the door.

"I *don't* ruin everything," Melody said.

"You shouldn't take anything he said seriously." Kristy put her arm around Melody.

"But Bill has had to stay home for almost a week now."

"That's a long time isn't it? Sometimes words hurt as much as pushing. But the words 'I'm sorry' can ease a lot of pain." Kristy raised her voice to make sure Bill heard what she was saying.

"I'm not going to apologize to her, so you can save your breath," Bill yelled through the door.

Kristy sighed. She needed to talk to the BSC members about this one. Maybe seven minds would be better than one. "Come on, Melody. You want to play Yahtzee?"

CHAPTER 9

"First Bill tried to talk me into letting Karen and David Michael come over to play even though he was grounded, then he said terrible things to Melody, then he refused to apologize." As soon as she called the meeting to order, Kristy had asked the rest of us what we thought was going on at the Kormans'.

"It sounds like a replay of what happened on Saturday. Although, that was physical. Bill pushed Melody and could have hurt her that day," Abby said.

"This was just words, but that can still be painful," Kristy reminded her.

At Kristy's comment, Mal looked up, then back down quickly. Words certainly could hurt, and Mal knew it.

"I'm supposed to baby-sit for Bill, Melody, and Skylar on Sunday afternoon," Mary Anne put in.

"Maybe what they need is something that

forces them to work together," Jessi suggested.

The rest of us nodded in agreement. *But what?* I wondered.

"We have until Sunday to come up with something. We'll all work on it and call you if we have any suggestions," Stacey said to Mary Anne.

"Great," she replied, sounding relieved.

I looked around at my friends, then cleared my throat. "How would you guys like to come to a party?" I asked.

"A party? Where?" asked Stacey.

"For what?" asked Jessi.

"What kind of party?" said Abby.

"Who'll be there?" Mal wanted to know. Everyone but her had sat up a little straighter and looked a little brighter when I asked the question.

"Right here, Saturday night, starting at seven and lasting until nine-thirty or so. Remember when I was trying to think of a way that you guys could get to know my seventh-grade friends a little better? That's what it's for."

"Sounds like fun," said Stacey.

"I've already talked to Shira, Joanna, and Jeannie. And Josh," I added. "They've all said they'll be here. I was waiting for the meeting to invite you guys. Do you think you'll be able to come?"

"Logan and I were planning to watch a

video on Saturday night at my house," said Mary Anne. "Could he come too? I mean, you don't want Josh to be the only boy."

"That's a good idea. Do you want to call him or should I?"

"I'll talk to him tonight," said Mary Anne.

"Have you told Shannon about the party?" asked Kristy.

"I'll call her." I picked up the list I'd been working on ever since Janine had said yes, and I added *call Shannon* after *rent a video* and *order pizza*.

"What about Anna?" Abby asked.

"Sure. Ask her," I said. "I'm leaving the asking up to you guys."

This would bring the total number of people to what? Ten or eleven? That was still a small group.

At six, everyone except Mary Anne and Stacey left. "Your parents agreed to let you have a party when they're out of town?" Stacey asked.

"They didn't say I couldn't, and Janine said it was okay," I replied.

"Janine said what was okay?" My sister stuck her head inside the doorway.

"That I could have a party tomorrow night," I said.

"I thought it sounded like fun." Janine

stepped inside the room and sat down in the director's chair. "Don't you guys?"

Mary Anne and Stacey nodded.

"I'm thinking about the food. What do you like to eat? I know Claudia will say chocolate, but what about everybody else?" Janine asked.

"I thought we'd have pizza," I reminded her.

"We can have pizza too, but what about dessert?" Janine said.

"You seem to have things pretty much under control," Stacey said, slipping her arms into her denim jacket and grabbing her backpack.

Mary Anne stood up too.

"But I could use help planning games. I wouldn't usually have games, but since the whole idea is for people to get acquainted, I thought games would be a way to break the ice," I said. I didn't want Stacey and Mary Anne to leave. They kept glancing at Janine, as if waiting for her to leave first. But Janine seemed to be glued to the chair.

"Games?" she mused. "I could develop a trivia game, perhaps. Something challenging but not too challenging."

"I think I may have enough games after all," I said quickly.

"I'll talk to you tomorrow," Stacey said to me. "Casual?"

"Definitely."

"And I'll invite Logan," said Mary Anne.

"Thanks. See you later." As Mary Anne and Stacey walked out of the room, the telephone rang. Janine and I reached for it at the same time, but she pulled back.

"Hi, Claudia. It's Peaches," my aunt said. "How are things going?"

"Good."

"Are you eating dinner?"

"Not yet. The BSC meeting just ended."

"BSC meeting? Even with your parents gone? Oh, well. I'm sure they thought of that before they left. Janine was home, wasn't she?"

"Yes, Janine was home." I looked at my sister and rolled my eyes. What had happened to my fun-loving aunt Peaches?

"Russ and I thought the two of you might like to join us tomorrow evening for dinner," Peaches continued.

"Dinner? Tomorrow? Saturday?" I stammered. "Um . . ."

"Claudia, ask Janine how she feels about coming over," Peaches said.

"It sounds like fun, but," I paused, "Janine and I were planning something . . . special. A sister thing."

Janine's head snapped up and she smiled at me, nodding and giving me a thumbs-up.

"You and Janine? A special *sister* thing?" I could hear the disbelief in her voice. Peaches and Mom are as different as Janine and I are.

"That's right. Me and Janine."

"That will be nice," said Peaches, sounding doubtful. "Have a good time. And be sure to . . ."

". . . call if we need anything," I said, finishing her sentence for her.

"All right. 'Bye."

I hung up the phone. "That was Peaches," I told Janine. "She wanted us to come over tomorrow night. I didn't think she needed to know about the party."

"I think you're correct. And the special sister thing sounded nice." Janine's eyes gleamed. "I'm feeling very excited about both your party *and* the special sister thing. What did you have in mind? Perhaps a sister slumber party?"

"Maybe," I said, not wanting to commit myself yet. "But Janine, let's concentrate on the party."

"Yes, first things first." She sailed out of the room.

I decided not to worry about what she might expect on the sister front. I had a party to plan. I needed to come up with some games. I wanted people to talk to one another, get acquainted. I could see how easy it would be for Josh, Shira, Joanna, and Jeannie to end up on one side of the room and the BSC members on the other — like boys and girls at sixth-grade dances. So how could I make sure everyone mixed?

I had some stickers in my desk. What if everyone received a sticker when he or she arrived and had to match it to a group of others? I found hearts, a page of animal stickers, and some stars. Three groups would be enough. All the hearts could be one team, the animals the second, and the stars the third. But what would each team do? If Janine really wanted to make some special food, she could create a giant cookie for each team to decorate.

Also, I could make up a list of facts about everybody at the party and people could try to match each fact to a person. That would be a start.

I started writing down facts:

I talk in my sleep. (Mal)
I live in a haunted house. (Mary Anne)
Carolyn Keene is my favorite author. (Me)
I love those Mets. (Logan)

This could be addictive, I thought as I wrote faster. By the time I finished, I had enough facts to keep everyone talking for days.

At dinner, Janine agreed to be in charge of the giant cookies. She suggested that we use some of the grocery money to buy decorations. She also said she'd type the facts (without the answers) on her computer and make copies for everyone the next day.

By the time I finally turned off my light and crawled into bed, I was so tired I thought I'd fall asleep immediately. But I couldn't. I was too excited. I looked at my clock. Only nineteen or so more hours until party time.

CHAPTER 10

"Claudia! You're not dressed yet." Janine came into my room wearing a pleated skirt, loafers, and a sweater. She moved toward the bed, then changed direction and lifted a pile of clothes off my desk chair, tossing them onto the bed.

"I'm still deciding," I said. "But at least I'm changing clothes."

"I changed," Janine replied, sounding hurt.

It was hard to tell with Janine. She had plenty of clothes, but most of them looked the same to me. Maybe she'd had on a navy skirt earlier and changed to black for this evening. Her sweater had a little bit of red trim and the one she had on earlier in the day had been a solid color. It wasn't a big change. On the other hand, I'd taken out several outfits, tried them on, and decided they weren't quite right for a hostess. I wished I had more time. I could have put together something special. All I had time

90

to do now was choose from what was in the closet . . . and in the dresser . . . and on the bed . . . plus the few things on the floor.

"Our guests will be arriving in a short while," Janine informed me, looking at her watch.

Our guests? "Janine, did you invite any of your friends to stop by?" I asked, thinking maybe I'd missed something.

"Of course not. This is a party for your friends, so that they may become better acquainted with one another. It will also give me an opportunity to get to know them better," she said. She picked up a red mohair sweater and laid it alongside a pair of black jeans. "Look, I have on red and black too. If you wear this, they could be the official hostess colors."

"But *I'm* the official hostess," I told her.

Janine looked me directly in the eye. "And *I'm* the official chaperone."

She had me there. I slipped into the black jeans, then pulled a black turtleneck over my head. I had a fleece top with turquoise, hot pink, and lime green stripes and one thin line of red. It was a boxy jacket style and looked festive, I decided.

"That's bright," Janine said as I buttoned the jacket.

I found a pair of earrings I'd made out of

91

curling ribbon and put them on, then stood back and looked at the results. Cool.

"The food is prepared. I have three large cookies for decorating later in the evening and a dozen sacked cookies for each member of the winning team. I've ordered pizza to be delivered at eight, and there's a variety of soda on ice in the cooler, plus the overflow is in the refrigerator. I also have chips and pretzels and even some fruit, should someone want a healthy alternative to the junk food." Janine ticked each item off on her fingers.

"Janine, you are the goddess of food and I thank you." I gave her a quick hug.

"You look terrific," Janine said. "Ready?"

"I think so." I pulled a brush through my hair one more time. I'd decided to wear it loose. "Josh and Stacey should be here in a few minutes to help set up."

As we ran down the stairs, the doorbell rang. Janine practically knocked me over in her rush to reach the door first.

"Stacey!" she said, throwing the door open. "I'm so delighted you could come. Enter!"

"Hi, Janine. Hi, Claud." Stacey stepped inside. "Josh is right behind me."

"Joshua, come right in," Janine called out the door. "It's party time."

I hugged Stacey. "I'm so excited," I whispered.

"Now, let's see what still needs to be done," Janine said as she closed the door behind Josh. I wiggled my fingers at him in greeting as he stood waiting for his instructions from the "official chaperone."

"Wait a minute," I said. "First you have to have a sticker." I peeled off a red heart for Josh (for obvious reasons) and a blue star for Stacey and stuck them on their shirts. For myself, I chose a pink heart. I wanted to be in Josh's group.

"What about me?" Janine asked.

After exchanging a glance with Stacey, I gave Janine a star.

"Stacey, you choose the music. Josh, you set out some of the napkins and plates that we'll need later for refreshments. Claudia, you start filling baskets and bowls with snacks," Janine said.

And, Queen Janine, what will you *be doing?* I wondered. She joined me in the kitchen. When the doorbell rang, she offered to take over and finish.

I wiped my hands quickly, then ran into the front hall. My first real guest. I opened the door. "Hi!" I said, with a big smile.

"Hi, yourself," Pete Black replied.

Pete Black? Had I invited Pete? He 's a good friend of Logan's, but I didn't remember even talking to him during the past week. He must have sensed my confusion, because he added, "Logan mentioned you were having a party and that it would be cool if I stopped by."

"Sure, the more the merrier," I said, quickly trying to figure out how many people that now meant. Twelve, maybe? That wasn't so many. I was "stickering" Pete with a squirrel to start the third group when I saw Emily Bernstein, another eighth-grade friend, coming up the walk with Erica Blumberg. Uh-oh. The word must have gotten out.

"Claudia, this is a great idea," Emily said, stepping inside.

"Thanks for inviting us," Erica added.

Janine had come into the hallway. She gave me a strange look but didn't say anything. Emily, Erica, Pete, and Stacey were chatting away while Josh looked on. I stuck a bear on Emily and a star on Erica, explaining that we'd be dividing into teams as soon as everyone arrived.

Before I could close the door, the Junk Bucket, Charlie Thomas's car, pulled up. Kristy climbed out, followed by Shannon, Abby, Anna, and Shannon's best friend from Stoneybrook Day, Greer Carson. I took a deep breath. This was a get-to-know-people party, after all. Still, I was starting to worry about whether we'd ordered enough pizza and if we had enough soda. Would three teams be enough?

And I hadn't included everybody in the trivia game!

I gave out stickers without really thinking about who should go where. Mary Anne and Logan arrived, followed by Rick Chow and Austin Bentley, two more friends of Logan's.

"What a crowd!" Mary Anne said, hesitating in the doorway.

"There are a few more people than I expected," I admitted. "And not everybody that I expect is here yet."

"You said to let our other friends know about the party," Mary Anne reminded me.

I didn't remember exactly what I'd said, but it obviously hadn't come out the way I'd meant it. I gave everyone in that group stickers too, then greeted Jeannie, Joanna, and Shira, who were followed by Mal and Jessi.

There was a solid wall of people around the table where we'd set out the food, as well as a crowd in the living room. I looked outside and saw no sign of other unexpected guests, so I closed the door. Someone turned the stereo up a notch. I started for the living room to turn it down again, then saw it was Janine adjusting the knobs. She was talking to Greer, who had on a star that matched Janine's.

In fact, when I settled down enough to notice, I realized that people were mixing with each other pretty well. Joanna was talking to

Kristy and Austin Bentley, while Shira was giggling with Emily and Jessi. Mal, Josh, and Mary Anne were sitting on the steps leading upstairs, deep in conversation — about what, I had no idea.

"Thanks for coming, everybody!" I shouted, wondering if I could be heard above all the noise. Janine rushed to my side, smiling. The noise level dropped a bit and a few people turned my way.

I raised my voice a little higher. "I gave out three kinds of stickers. Find the other people who are wearing the same kind you are. They're your team members."

I took a deep breath. It was much quieter as people moved to find their teammates. They stood in silent clumps, looking at me. I caught Josh's eye and he smiled, making me feel better. "I'm going to pass out sheets with trivia facts about some of the people here. You'll need to talk to each other to find who the fact is about."

Pete said something I couldn't hear and everyone around him laughed.

"The winning team will be the one which correctly identifies the most people," I added.

Janine handed me the sheets she'd typed up, and I passed them out. There were exactly enough. Janine must have made extras. "Let the games begin," Janine added.

"I thought there were going to be fourteen people here," Janine said quietly to me. "I count twenty and with me, twenty-one. I didn't really think we'd use all those sheets."

Twenty-one. That sounded like a lot. I had thought eleven or twelve people would show up.

"I ordered pizza for fifteen," Janine continued.

"We'll make it stretch," I replied.

"The snacks are almost completely gone already," Janine pointed out, "and I figured on two sodas per person."

I squirmed a little.

"Where did the extra people come from?" Janine asked. "How could you have been so far off on your total?"

I was more worried about stretching the food than about exactly how many people were present. After all they were here and they weren't going to leave.

"We still have the giant cookies," I reminded her. "And everybody's probably eaten dinner so they won't be that hungry."

"People do seem to be having fun," Janine observed. "I guess it's all right. I think I'll try to match person with fact."

I smiled. "Okay," I said. I headed for the den. The star team was already there, filling out their sheets.

"Is there a prize?" Rick called to me as I passed his group in the living room.

"First choice at pizza," I said.

"I hope you ordered sausage and bacon. We're ripping through these questions."

"Claudia, no fair if you work with your team. You know all the answers," said Kristy from the dining room.

"That's right," yelled Pete, "no fair."

"I promise I won't help anybody," I assured them.

Then I heard it and my heart practically stopped — the sound of breaking glass coming from the direction of the living room.

CHAPTER 11

Either Janine was faster than me, or she was already in the room when it happened, because she was on her knees picking up pieces of the shattered vase when I arrived — along with just about everyone else in the room.

"Be careful of the broken glass," Josh warned me.

Mal was standing back, staring at Janine and the vase, her face bright red and her eyes shiny with tears. "I'm so sorry," she said, "I'm so sorry. I'm such a klutz."

Why couldn't it have been anyone other than Mal? I thought.

Jessi hurried to Mal's side and put an arm around her. Stacey, Abby, Kristy, and Mary Anne squeezed through the crowd to join her too, reminding her that it was an accident.

"Maybe you can glue it back together," Logan suggested.

"I don't think so," Janine said, shaking her head.

"It's just a vase," I said, trying to convince myself as well as everyone else. "Don't worry about it." Still, I could barely stand to look at all the tiny pieces scattered over the floor. What would Mom and Dad say?

"You are absolutely correct, Claudia," Janine said, standing up. "We'll clean this up so that no one is injured, and it will be fine." She smiled weakly.

"I'll clean it up," Mal offered.

"Let me show you where the broom and dustpan are kept." Janine led her into the kitchen.

The doorbell rang. I wondered who hadn't yet shown up.

Joanna, Kristy, and Austin were standing at the open front door by the time I reached it, each one holding a pizza box.

"We need money," Kristy called to me.

I wove my way through the crowd again and found the money Janine had set aside for pizza. By the time I'd paid for it, the only thing left was a slice of Canadian bacon and pineapple. I decided to wait for cookies.

"Here, I saved you a piece." Josh appeared at my side and handed me a slice of pepperoni. I bit into it and kept walking.

"Claudia," he called after me. "Come in here with me for awhile."

"Can't," I said with my mouth full. I kept walking.

Mal and Jessi were still in the living room, cleaning up the glass. Joanna and Jeannie had taken up a spot on the steps, while Austin, Rick, Pete, and Logan were watching sports news on the TV. What had happened to the teams?

"Claudia, could you please join me in the kitchen?" Janine yelled through the crowd.

"What's wrong?" I asked when I'd fought my way to the door.

"We have depleted the food supply," Janine announced.

"We still have cookies," I said.

"But I've had several requests for more pizza. If we'd only known *exactly* how many guests . . ."

It was too late to worry about that. I'd thought I knew how many.

"What do we have on hand? I'll bet we can find something." I pulled open the pantry door. There was an unopened jar of hearts of palm, some pineapple, tomato sauce, and a can of beans.

"There's frozen pizza dough," Janine said.

"Then we'll make our own pizza." I pulled

the cans out of the pantry and lined them up on the counter. "It takes, what, ten or fifteen minutes to cook?"

"We haven't got any mozzarella cheese." I joined Janine in front of the fridge.

There were, however, a few slices of American cheese. "We can use this. It'll be a Kishi special."

"I'll see what I can do." Janine turned on the oven and took out our pizza pan.

I found some carrots and a carton of health-dip in the refrigerator. I scraped the health-dip into a bowl and cut up the carrots. There was also cold spaghetti, but I didn't think that would interest anyone.

"Maybe the smaller cookies should be dessert rather than a prize," I said.

Janine slipped her pizza into the oven. "Announce the cookie-decorating competition now. It's becoming very noisy in there."

I'd been so busy trying to figure out what to feed everyone that I hadn't noticed the noise. Now, however, I realized the party was much louder than it had been.

I picked up the three giant cookies and the decorating supplies that Janine had collected and carried them into the dining room. Shira, Stacey, and Rick were walking around balancing pizza boxes on their heads. I checked to make sure there weren't any breakables around.

Mal and Jessi were still in the living room. The glass was cleaned up, and they were sitting on the sofa, talking. "We're going to decorate cookies now. Find your team," I said. They looked up and nodded but kept talking.

In the den, another group, led by Shannon, was singing what sounded like camp songs. "Cookie time," I said, "in the dining room." The boys in the group immediately jumped up and ran for the door.

Before I could explain that the cookies were for decorating, Austin had broken one and was handing out the pieces.

"I love these!" I heard Anna say. She opened a jar of colored sprinkles and poured some into her hand.

"Let me try some," said Erica, taking the jar.

"Icing in a spray can!" Pete squirted some into his mouth.

"That's gross," Kristy said, grabbing it.

"I didn't put my mouth on it," Pete said. "It's good. Have some." He reached for the can and pressed the nozzle, causing a line of icing to ooze out onto Kristy's arm.

"Yuck!" she said, but she licked it off.

"The icing tastes good on cookies too," said Abby. She took the can from Kristy and sprayed some on a piece of cookie, then ate it.

Emily took one of the icing cans and made a face on a cookie. Abby tried to press red hots into a cookie and it broke, sending pieces shooting across the dining room table.

"Hockey!" yelled Pete, sliding the biggest piece back. Others joined in, and cookies flew back and forth and onto the floor.

I looked for Janine, wishing the "official chaperone" would step in and help me get the party back on track.

"What's wrong?" Josh was at my elbow.

"It's a little crazy in there," I said, trying not to sound too worried. "Where's Janine?"

"I saw her going upstairs with Shira and some other people a few minutes ago," Josh said. "Want me to go find her?"

The timer on the oven buzzed. "Would you take the pizza out of the oven?" I asked Josh. "I'll find Janine." I ran upstairs.

Janine was in her bedroom in front of the computer. Shira, Joanna, and Jeannie were leaning close to the screen as Janine showed them something. They were supposed to be mixing with my BSC friends! What were they doing up here?

"Janine?" I said from the doorway. She looked over her shoulder. "Can you come downstairs?"

"We'll be finished here in a minute," she said. The group broke into laughter as something moved across the screen.

"But Janine —"

104

"Claudia, I said in a minute. Relax and enjoy your guests."

Easy for her to say. I hadn't had a chance to talk to anybody. And I'd totally ignored Josh.

I heard the sound of a television and realized someone was in my parents' bedroom. I rushed to the end of the hall. "Hey, guys, you need to go back downstairs," I said to Rick, Pete, and Erica. "You can watch TV in the den."

"But Logan made us turn this off down there, because Mary Anne wanted to watch a movie," said Rick. "This is the death match of the WWF and I don't want to miss it."

"This bedroom is off-limits," I said in a firm voice.

The TV screen went black and the three of them filed out.

I closed the door to Mom and Dad's room, then pulled the door to my room shut as I passed by. Downstairs, Shannon and Abby were playing "keep the cookie away from Anna in the hallway," while the hockey game was still going on in the dining room. I reached up and grabbed the "keep-away cookie" out of the air and ate it.

"Hey!" said Shannon.

"There are breakables here." I pointed at a lamp on the table.

The hockey game had divided itself into two teams, each with a cheering squad. They'd even moved the chairs out of the way. I slipped through them into the kitchen, thinking that if I brought the pizza out it might distract everyone.

Josh was standing by the counter with a funny look on his face. "What's the matter?" I asked.

"The pizza," he said. "I don't think the American cheese . . . um . . . worked."

"Thanks for your help," I said sarcastically, taking a look at the pizza. He was right — it was a disaster.

"What's going on in here?" Joanna appeared at the door to the kitchen. "Josh? What's wrong?" Jeannie and Shira crowded in beside her.

"Nothing," Josh said, turning his back on me and joining them. "Let's go in the other room."

I closed my eyes and counted to ten. I shouldn't have been so abrupt with Josh. I was starting to think I shouldn't have had a party.

At that moment the doorbell rang. Maybe the pizza man had forgotten to leave a large pepperoni. I was sure that would do the trick.

I passed Janine, who was holding up a cookie and explaining something to Pete Black, on my way to the front door. Pete had a dazed look on his face. I'll bet he had no idea what Janine was talking about.

"Claudia, where's the new Blade record?" Stacey called as I opened the door.

"In a minute," I answered, then turned to see who had arrived late, hoping they weren't expecting food.

Instead, I found Peaches, Russ, and Lynn.

CHAPTER 12

"Peaches!" Her name came out as a squeak. Meanwhile, Russ's and Peaches's mouths were hanging open, and they kept blinking their eyes as if they thought what they saw might eventually disappear.

I turned, looking for Janine. She still held the cookie in the air. Then she swallowed, handed the cookie to Pete, and walked toward us. From the corner of my eye, I saw Stacey grab Mary Anne and Kristy. The three of them spread out and walked among the kids, talking in low voices.

Peaches began to speak, and the room suddenly fell quiet. "Tell me I don't see what I think I see," she said.

I heard rustling behind me, but no one said anything.

"Peaches, it probably looks worse than it is," Russ said.

Lynn grinned and reached out to me.

"Girls, I'd like an explanation," Peaches said in a voice that reminded me of Mom.

"It's only a few people," Janine said.

"Mom and Dad didn't say we couldn't have friends over," I added.

"This is what you call a special sister activity, Claudia?" Peaches was hurt that we — that I — had lied to her.

"Maybe we should come inside and discuss this after everyone has gone home," Russ said in a calm voice.

"After everyone has gone?" I repeated.

"I think it's time for your guests to leave," said Russ.

Peaches, clutching Lynn tightly, stalked into the living room.

"Who needs a ride home?" Russ called into the dining room.

"I'll call Charlie," I heard Kristy say to Abby.

Pete, Austin, and Rick were already at the door. They lived close, so they'd be picked up soon.

"Thanks, Claudia," Pete said, and the other boys echoed what he'd said.

Joanna, Shira, and Jeannie were next.

"We'll see you at school on Monday," Jeannie said.

"Thanks for the pizza," Shira said to Janine.

"And everything," Joanna added.

"Glad you could come," Janine said vaguely.

Both of us kept looking at Peaches in the living room. Mal and Jessi were playing with Lynn while Peaches watched, not a trace of a smile on her face.

Emily and Erica left quietly once Erica's dad arrived. In fact, everything was too quiet, especially considering how loud it had been before my aunt and uncle showed up.

"Do you want us to stay and help you clean up?" Stacey asked. Mary Anne and Abby nodded, indicating that they'd stay too.

The dining room floor was covered with cookie crumbs. Logan joined us in the hallway, crunching with each step. There were paper plates and napkins everywhere. Someone had taken the empty soda cans and built a pyramid on the kitchen counter. Dining room chairs were in the living room, and the ottoman usually in the living room was missing. Even though I knew it would take Janine and me from now until our parents came home to clean up properly — I swallowed hard when I thought about Mom and Dad and what they were going to say — I shook my head.

A horn honked out front. Charlie had arrived in record time. Kristy, Abby, Anna, Shannon, and Greer ran to the car, quiet until they reached the end of the walk, then talking as soon as the car doors opened.

"Mary Anne and I can stay to help," Stacey said again.

"You kids better go home," Russ said.

Josh appeared from the rear of the house, a serious expression on his face. I remembered yelling at him in the kitchen before Peaches arrived. Our eyes met, but I couldn't tell what he was thinking.

"I'll stay and help," Josh offered in a quiet voice.

"Thanks," I said. Then I caught Russ's eye and he shook his head, so I added, "But you'd better go too."

"Talk to you tomorrow," Stacey whispered, giving me a quick hug, then followed Mary Anne, Logan, Mal, and Jessi down the sidewalk. Mrs. Pike would give them a ride home.

Josh was the last one out the door. He stopped, then turned around and wiggled his fingers at me. I tried to smile.

Janine was sitting in the living room, across from Peaches and Lynn. Russ sat down beside Peaches. I felt all of them looking at me as I walked into the room and sank to the floor near Janine's chair.

"I couldn't believe my eyes. You two, my nieces, and a houseful of out-of-control kids . . ." Peaches began.

"They weren't out of control," Janine said,

but a piercing glare from Peaches shut her up.

Lynn held her arms out to me and I scooted forward to take her, but Peaches pulled her back.

"Your parents may not have said that you couldn't invite friends over while they were gone," Peaches said, turning to me, "but I'm sure they never dreamed, Claudia, that you'd invite over the entire student body of Stoneybrook Middle School."

"It was just the kids in the BSC, some of my seventh-grade friends, and . . ." I began to say, but one look from Peaches shut me right up. This was a side of my aunt I'd never seen.

"What was Mallory saying about a broken vase?" Peaches asked.

"She knocked a vase from a table," Janine said.

"It's a new vase. I'll buy Mom a replacement," I added.

"It's the only thing that was permanently damaged," Janine added.

Looking around, it was hard to believe that.

"And Janine — allowing Claudia to have a party when your parents are out of town, taking part in the activities, even. I cannot believe you acted in such an irresponsible manner." Peaches shook her head and pulled Lynn closer.

"Are you going to tell Mom and Dad?" Janine asked without looking up.

112

Peaches sighed loudly. "I wish I didn't have to."

"But you are?" I asked.

"We are." Peaches looked at Russ and they nodded.

I swallowed hard. Mom and Dad were going to be more disappointed than Peaches and Russ, if that were possible.

"We didn't expect to be here longer than a minute. I wanted to see what a special sister evening consisted of. Little did I know," Peaches said, rising. "My advice to you girls is to clean up the house, spotlessly, and hope that your parents take your efforts into consideration when they're deciding how to handle things."

"Okay," Janine said softly.

"You're both to stay right here until your mother and father come home tomorrow," Peaches went on.

"Are we grounded?" I asked.

Peaches hesitated. "Yes."

"We have to get Lynn to bed," Russ said.

"Could I give her a kiss good-bye?" I asked.

Peaches nodded.

"I'm very sorry," I heard Janine say to our aunt and uncle as I cuddled Lynn for a few moments.

"We'll talk to you tomorrow," Russ said as they pulled the front door closed.

Janine and I sat in total silence for a few moments.

"I'll start cleaning in the living room," I said as soon as I heard the car pull away.

"Fine," Janine said, her voice as cold as Peaches's had been. "I'll be in the kitchen. The first order of business is to rid the premises of that disgusting pizza."

I walked around, looking for pieces of furniture that belonged in the living room. I was pushing the ottoman in from the den when Janine called to me.

"Where is the pizza?"

"The last thing I heard, Josh had tried it. He looked as if he might throw up," I said.

"Surely those children didn't eat it all!" The clatter of pots and pans drowned out anything else Janine might have said.

Children? We weren't children. We were teenagers, not that much younger than Janine.

Janine was up to her elbows in dishwater when I marched into the kitchen. "We aren't children, you know," I began.

"You aren't? That's what you acted like here tonight — immature children. I should have known that I couldn't trust a group of *children* to behave. Your friends have no sense of D-E-C-O-R-U-M."

"Don't spell at me! Does your sense of *decorum* include trying so hard to make my friends like you that you can't act like the 'official chaperone' you said you were going to be?"

"Not one guest showed an ounce of responsibility. Would they act the way they acted here in their own homes?" Janine demanded.

"You did. Were you responsible? Peaches doesn't think so," I said hotly.

"And I guess you were!" Janine pulled the plug in the sink and there was a huge sucking noise as the dishwater flowed into the drain.

I turned and left the kitchen, crunching my way through the dining room.

"What are you going to tell Mom and Dad about the vase?" Janine was right behind me.

"That it's broken," I said, tired of arguing with her.

"Broken because you invited so many of your friends."

"You only wish you had friends to invite to a party," I said.

Janine's mouth snapped shut and she backed away from me, then turned and stalked out of the room.

I knew that was a mean thing to say. I wished I could take it back. "Janine!" I called. She acted as if she hadn't heard me. I called again. Then the vacuum cleaner roared to life, drowning out my voice.

I sighed, grabbed a trash bag, and started stuffing it full of paper plates and napkins.

So much for this party solving all my problems.

CHAPTER 13

Sunday

Thank you, Jessi!
Your suggestion was
perfect. Bill and Melody
did a great job together.
They solved an enormous
problem. Who cares if
it purposely created
the problem in the
first place?

Finally, some good news from the Korman battleground. At the Monday BSC meeting Mary Anne filled us in on how her sitting job had gone.

"Bill is still grounded," Mrs. Korman said as soon as Mary Anne arrived on Sunday.

Mary Anne was holding Skylar as Mr. and Mrs. Korman prepared to leave for an afternoon movie. "It's such a nice day. Is it okay if Bill plays outside?" she asked.

"Certainly," Mr. Korman answered. "Just keep an eye on him and Melody."

Mary Anne nodded, remembering everything that Kristy and Abby had told her.

"We'll be home by dinnertime," said Mrs. Korman. And then they were gone.

Still carrying Skylar, Mary Anne went upstairs to say hi to Melody and Bill. She knocked on Melody's door first.

"Hi, Melody. It's Mary Anne. Everything okay in there?"

Melody opened her door a crack and peeked through. "Is Bill out there?" she whispered.

"He's in his room," Mary Anne said, realizing things were worse than she'd expected. "Why?"

The door opened a little wider. "Bill is an old meanie," Melody said, her eyes filling with tears. "At lunch he said that I was dumb and stupid and wouldn't ever learn multiplication. We haven't even had multiplication in school yet. Could you help me learn?"

"We can work on that later. It's warm outside today and I thought we'd take Skylar for a walk. Does that sound like fun?" Mary Anne asked.

Melody nodded slowly. "What about Bill? Is he going too? He's grounded."

"Your mom and dad said he could play outside if he wanted to," Mary Anne said.

"If he's going . . ." Melody hesitated.

"Let's give it a try. Maybe a walk is just what we all need."

Melody still looked uncertain.

"Bill might not even want to go. Let me talk to him. You find a jacket and meet us downstairs. In fact, could you find a jacket for Skylar too?"

"Sure," Melody replied. "May I push the stroller?"

Mary Anne smiled and nodded. She shifted Skylar to a more comfortable position and moved down the hall to Bill's room.

"Hey, Bill! It's Mary Anne," she called as she rapped on his door.

The door flew open. "I knew you were here. I heard Mom and Dad telling you I was still grounded," Bill said, scowling.

"But you can go for a walk with us if you

want. Your parents said that would be okay."

Bill looked over his shoulder. Mary Anne could see tiny action figures spread all over the floor. "I'm sort of in the middle of something."

"The plan is for all of us to go," Mary Anne said firmly.

Bill started to close the door, but Mary Anne grabbed it. "You can walk on one side of me and Melody can walk on the other. You don't have to talk to each other at all. You can talk to me instead. Have you ever heard anyone say that if you can't say something nice, you shouldn't say anything at all? We can use that as a rule for conversation between you and Melody today."

"Then I won't have anything at all to say to her," Bill said.

"Okay, sounds like a plan," Mary Anne replied. "Find a jacket and meet us outside."

Mary Anne scribbled a note saying they were going for a walk around the block, in case Mr. and Mrs. Korman returned early. Then she stuck a key in her jeans pocket, and zipped up her jacket. Melody joined her, carrying Skylar's jacket, and handed Skylar a set of plastic keys. A play steering wheel was attached to the stroller, and Skylar pretended to put the keys into the ignition. Then she dropped them into the stroller seat and grabbed the steering wheel, making motor noises.

119

Bill finally arrived and stood a few feet away from the girls.

"Ready?" Mary Anne asked. He nodded.

Mary Anne checked to make sure the lock on the doorknob was turned, then pulled the door tightly shut. "Let's walk around the block," she suggested.

Melody grabbed the stroller handle and took off. Mary Anne stayed behind with Bill. People were out in their yards, raking leaves. Pickup ballgames were going on. Bill walked a little slower each time they passed one.

"Hey, Bill! We could use a third baseman," David Michael yelled when they walked by the Thomas/Brewer house.

Bill looked up at Mary Anne and she shook her head.

"Can't right now," he yelled back, then stuck his hands in his pockets. Mary Anne watched the muscles in his jaw tighten as he stared at Melody walking ahead of them. But he didn't say anything.

When they turned the corner to head back to the Kormans', Skylar started fussing.

"I think it's time for her juice," said Melody, "then her nap."

"We'll be home in a minute," Mary Anne said. "Thanks, Bill, for not arguing about staying to play with David Michael," she said in a low voice.

"I wanted to," Bill said with a shadow of a smile.

Melody pulled the stroller close to the back door and started to unfasten the straps around Skylar.

Mary Anne stuck her hand into her coat pocket. "Hold on," she said. "Where's the key? I put it right here in my pocket." She tried the back door, but it wouldn't open. Then she pulled her pocket inside out. "Oh, no! There's a huge hole in it! The key must have fallen out."

Melody scrambled to her feet, leaving Skylar sitting in the middle of the patio, her cries growing louder by the minute. "Bill, go see if the front door is locked too."

Bill ran around the side of the house while Melody tried the garage door. She entered through the side but came out again, shaking her head. "The door to the house is locked," she said.

Mary Anne picked up Skylar and settled in a patio chair, rocking her until she quieted.

When Bill returned, he was shaking his head too. "Locked up tight," he announced. "I knew it would be." He looked at Melody.

"What are we going to do?" Melody asked.

"I've managed to quiet Skylar, so I hate to move. What about checking the windows?" Mary Anne suggested.

Bill and Melody talked quietly, then Bill headed to the front of the house, while Melody took off around the other side.

Skylar felt heavy, and when Mary Anne looked down, she realized that she had fallen asleep.

After awhile, Bill and Melody returned together, their heads close. Mary Anne put her finger against her lips as they approached, then pointed to Skylar.

"Maybe we should get the ladder and see if any of the windows upstairs are open," Bill whispered.

"That's a good idea, but maybe you should try to find the key first. It must have dropped out someplace along the way. You could walk together along the route we took," Mary Anne said.

"I'll look on one side of the sidewalk and you can look on the other," Bill said to Melody.

"We'll find it, Mary Anne," Melody said as they left together. "Don't worry."

Mary Anne smiled. She wasn't a bit worried.

As soon as Bill and Melody were far enough away, Mary Anne held Skylar in one arm, then eased her free hand into her jeans pocket, and dug out the key. She tossed it gently into Skylar's stroller, then settled back to wait for the kids to return.

After a few minutes, Bill and Melody reappeared. As they walked around the side of the house, they examined the ground carefully. When they reached Mary Anne, they sat in lawn chairs nearby. "We didn't find it," Bill said.

"But we have another plan," Melody added, looking at her brother.

"We know that it's not the best idea, but we don't think Mom and Dad will mind that much." Bill leaned forward. "We'll break the glass in the back door, reach inside, and unlock it. That way you can put Skylar to bed."

"And we can go to the bathroom," said Melody, wriggling in the chair.

Mary Anne pretended to consider the plan. She chewed on her lip for awhile, then nodded. "I guess that's what we'll have to do. Why don't the two of you take Skylar's stroller to the garage and put it away, then try to find something we can use to break the glass in the window."

"I saw this on TV once," said Bill. "The guy took his shoe and wrapped it in a towel."

"What about a hammer?" suggested Melody. "We don't have to be quiet or anything."

"The main thing is that we don't want anyone to end up hurt by the broken glass," Mary Anne put in.

"Right. I'll do it with a hammer," Bill said to Melody.

They rose together and Melody grabbed the handle of the stroller. As she whirled it around, the key fell off the seat and clattered onto the cement patio.

"Oh, man!" Bill smacked himself across the forehead with his hand. "We should have looked in the stroller."

"Skylar loves keys," said Melody, leaning down to pick it up.

"At least we found it before we broke the window," Bill said to his sister. She nodded.

Mary Anne told me later that she wanted to say something about how well they'd worked together, but she hesitated to break the spell that had settled over them. They were even laughing about how hard it was to see things right in front of them.

Melody unlocked the door and held it open for Mary Anne, Bill, and Skylar.

After Skylar was settled in her crib, still asleep, Mary Anne hurried downstairs to find Bill and Melody in the kitchen spreading peanut butter on crackers and pouring juice for the three of them.

They were finishing their snack when Mr. and Mrs. Korman arrived.

"It's very quiet in here," Mrs. Korman said, her eyes fixed on Bill and Melody sitting side by side at the kitchen counter.

"Skylar is napping," Mary Anne said, "and we're finishing up our snack. We've been on a walk — together."

"Together?" Mr. Korman asked.

Bill looked at his empty plate, then at his sister. "You had some good ideas when we were locked out of the house," he mumbled. "I guess you're not so dumb after all." He paused, then continued, "I'm sorry I've been so mean, Melody. I'll try to be nicer." He looked sideways at his parents.

Mr. and Mrs. Korman beamed.

"Thank you, Bill. I accept your apology," Melody said in a very grown-up voice.

"Let's go play rescue nine-one-one upstairs in my room. You can be the dispatcher and I'll be the firefighter trying to help the mom escape from the locked house," Bill said to Melody. "Is that okay?" he asked his parents.

"Fine. Or you could play outside for a little longer if you want. I thought I saw David Michael and Karen in their yard when we drove by. Maybe they'd like to join you," said Mr. Korman.

"You mean I'm not grounded anymore?" A big smile appeared on Bill's face.

"As long as you are considerate of your sister . . ."

"Come on, Melody, let's tell David Michael how we rescued Mary Anne."

The Kormans turned to Mary Anne and she began to explain.

CHAPTER 14

"Claudia, wake up! We still have cleaning to do before Mom and Dad come home." Janine was leaning over my bed, shaking my shoulder.

"What time is it?" I mumbled, pulling the blankets over my head.

"Time to rise and shine. Right now. I'm not going to pick up your mess all by myself," Janine said.

I threw back the covers. "But I'm sure you have some good ideas about how I should do it." I climbed out of bed, stretched, and looked around for something to put on.

"This is what you need to do: Clean up the dining room, making sure that you remove every cookie crumb, then vacuum the front hallway, and clean all the debris from the den."

"And what will you be doing?" I asked, yawning.

"I'm going to fix a special dinner for Mom

and Dad." She turned and began to leave my room.

The dinner sounded like a good idea, but I wasn't going to tell her that. I looked at the clock. It was early. I wondered if Josh was up yet. I felt awful about yelling at him. I reached for the phone.

"Claudia," Janine said sharply.

I froze.

"No speaking on the telephone. Stick to the task at hand."

"Yes, ma'am," I said. She left before I could salute.

As soon as I dressed, I went downstairs. Janine was in the kitchen hunched over a cookbook.

The dining room was the most visibly wrecked. Every step I took crunched. Crumbs followed me into the kitchen as I grabbed the broom and dustpan out of the closet — neither looking at nor speaking to my sister.

After I swept, I returned to the kitchen to empty the dustpan. Janine passed by me as if I weren't there.

In the den, I found the garbage bag I'd left there the night before and started gathering the remaining trash. The living room needed vacuuming. I turned on the stereo in the den loudly enough so that I could hear it in the next room. I was dancing around, picking up trash to the sounds of Blade, when I ran into Janine standing in the middle of the room, her hands on her hips.

She turned and walked out of the room. The music ended abruptly.

I rushed to the den. "Why did you do that?" I asked.

"You're to concentrate on work," Janine informed me.

I wanted to say "You're not the boss of me," but Janine didn't give me a chance. She was gone before I could open my mouth.

I threw trash into the bag until it wouldn't hold any more, then twisted it tightly closed, thinking of Janine's neck as I did.

The doorbell rang. I wondered if answering the door was off-limits for me too? When Janine didn't answer it, I did. I looked out the peephole and saw Stacey on the porch holding a bag. She waved at me.

"Hi! I didn't expect to see you today," I greeted her, standing back so she could come inside.

"We have something for you." Stacey held out the bag.

"What is it?" I slowly opened it. Inside was a vase identical to the one that had been broken the night before. I pulled it out. "This is wonderful! Where did you find it?"

"I thought I remembered seeing the vase in a

store downtown. After the party, we felt bad that you were in trouble with your aunt and uncle, and we knew that the broken vase was only going to make things worse. I called everybody and we all agreed to chip in to pay for a new vase and I volunteered to bring it to you."

I hugged Stacey. "The BSC is the best!" I said.

"Not only the BSC," Stacey said. "Joanna, Jeannie, Shira, and Josh want to contribute too. So do Greer, Rick, Austin, Pete, Emily, and Erica."

I stared at the vase. It would be a permanent reminder of how wonderful my friends were, and how they could work together.

"We talked about coming over to help you clean up, but we weren't sure that Janine would let us," Stacey said in a low voice.

"You're right about that. I can't talk on the phone or watch television or anything." I looked toward the kitchen. I was waiting for Janine to come and chase Stacey away.

"If you have a chance to call, I'll be home later," Stacey said.

"Thanks again," I replied, keeping a tight hold on the vase.

Stacey ran out to her car. Mrs. McGill waved as I shut the door.

"Who was that?" Janine asked.

"Stacey. Look." I held the vase out for my sister to see.

"Hmmph!" Again, she turned around and walked away.

"Janine! They went to a lot of trouble to find the vase and bring it to us. They were worried about what Mom and Dad would say — "

"They were worried you'd be in trouble," Janine interrupted.

I set the vase on the table in the hallway. I'd take it into the living room in a minute, after I carried the trash bag outside. I opened the front door.

"Where do you think you're going now?" Janine demanded.

I whirled around — and heard a sickening sound as the vase hit the ground.

Janine and I jumped back at the same time. The vase twirled, rocked, then lay there, still in one piece. I dropped the trash bag and picked up the vase, searching for cracks and chips.

"Is it okay?" Janine asked in a whisper.

I nodded, then let out the breath I'd been holding. When I finally faced my sister, she was massaging her forehead, her eyes closed.

"Janine, what is going on with you?" I asked. "You haven't been the same since you and Jerry broke up, which was a good thing, remember? He wasn't right for you. Why are you still acting so weird?"

Janine sat down on the hall floor, running her fingers through her hair. "You're right about Jerry. But he was my boyfriend for quite awhile and we spent most of our free time together. I lost touch with my other friends and I don't know how to reconnect with those people." She clasped her hands in her lap and looked at me.

I couldn't help smiling a little. "Why don't you throw a party?" I asked.

We laughed together, then Janine reached out and gave me — and the vase — a quick hug. I realized I could have been more sensitive to what Janine was experiencing, if I hadn't been so wrapped up in my own problems. Maybe now we could come up with some ideas — together.

My first suggestion was a special sister activity.

"I'd like that, Claudia," Janine replied. Her eyes glowed. "We'll discuss the details later. But, I'd like to know more about art."

"And I'd like to know more about computers," I admitted.

We were still in the hall, brainstorming ways that Janine might reestablish some of her old friendships, when Mom and Dad opened the door.

Mom looked at the big bag of trash, then at Janine, then at me. "Hello, girls," she said.

I pulled the trash bag behind me. "Mom, Dad, you're back!"

We exchanged hugs all around.

"Did you have fun?" Janine asked.

"It was a wonderful conference," Mom said.

"And so good to see the Simpsons," Dad added. "I can't remember when I've eaten as much as we did the last few days." He patted his stomach.

"And what about you two?" Mom asked, looking at the bag again, then at the vase I still held.

"There's something we need to tell you," I said quickly, and Janine moved a little closer, nodding.

Mom's eyes darted nervously between us.

"Everything is all right," Janine assured her. "But, well, last night I agreed that Claudia could have a few friends over."

"I wanted my BSC friends and my seventh-grade friends to have a chance to get better acquainted," I said. "But I wasn't very clear about who was invited, and a few more people showed up than we expected."

"Things never went truly out of control," Janine continued, "but it was loud and messy . . . and a vase was broken." I held up the new one.

"Claudia's friends replaced it," Janine said.

Mom's and Dad's expressions grew serious

as they looked from me to Janine and back to me.

"Russ and Peaches stopped by and they, um, weren't happy," I said.

"They thought we were being irresponsible," said Janine.

"And we were." Janine and I nodded.

"I'm surprised at you, Janine," Mom said.

"And a little disappointed," Dad added.

"There was no . . . drinking involved, was there?" Mom looked at the trash bag again.

"Nothing like that at all. They ate a lot. Pizza, soda, cookies, that sort of thing. No drinking," Janine stressed.

"I'm glad you told us about it. I don't think I would have known from looking at the house. It's very neat." Mom walked through to the kitchen and everyone followed.

"What's that smell?" Dad asked.

"I took one of Mom's casseroles out of the freezer and put it in the oven so it would be ready when you returned. I wanted to prepare something special, but there wasn't much left to eat," Janine explained.

"You seem well aware that what you did was wrong." Mom opened the oven door and peeked inside.

"And it was," Dad emphasized.

I waited, still clutching the vase, for what

they were going to say next — what our punishment would be.

"Still, we can't have something like this happen again." Dad looked at Janine, then at me. "Mom and I will discuss your punishment and let you know later. Why don't you finish cleaning up while we unpack?"

"Thanks, Dad," Janine said.

"Glad you're back," I said.

Janine grabbed the big bag of trash she'd gathered from the kitchen, and I grabbed the one in the front hallway. Then we took them outside together.

CHAPTER 15

"I tried to call you last night."

I whirled around and came face-to-face with Josh. I stuffed my backpack inside the locker and stood in front of it. "I know. I'm not allowed to use the telephone this week except for official BSC business. Mom and Dad were a little upset about the party."

"I guess they weren't the only ones." Josh looked away.

"I know I yelled at you and I'm sorry. I even asked Mom if I could call and tell you that, but she said no. That whole night was a little out of control," I admitted.

"I guess." Josh shrugged. "See you later." He wandered off.

Oh, well. It would give me a chance to carry out the surprise I'd spent the evening working on.

I headed for Josh's locker. As soon as I made sure he wasn't anyplace nearby, I opened the locker and stuck in the candy flower bouquet I'd put together. I'd used up a major part of my junk food stash to create my masterpiece. Hershey Kisses were bunched together to form silver flower buds on top of licorice stems with candy bar leaves. Then I dug out the certificates Janine had helped me create on the computer. I'd made three "Claudia Time Certificates," each one redeemable for an afternoon of quality time — Josh and me only. I wasn't sure he'd take me up on the offer. But I wanted to try.

I closed the locker door, then, using the wrapping paper and ribbon I'd brought from home, I decorated the outside to look like a gift package. I'd barely had time to admire my work when the bell rang and I had to rush to my first class.

I didn't see Josh all day. After school I hung around my locker, waiting for him to show up. My backpack was loaded and I'd slung it over my shoulder when he appeared.

"Hi," I said, smiling.

Josh was holding one of the certificates, and the red ribbon was hanging around his neck, but he wasn't smiling.

"What's up?" I asked, my smile fading.

"Exactly how do I redeem this certificate?"

"For when?"

"This afternoon?" Josh asked, looking at me out of the corner of his eye.

I cleared my throat.

"If you can't —" Josh began.

"Excuse me, sir, but I would be happy to re-deem this certificate for an afternoon of Claudia time. That will involve a short trip to Donut Express followed by a delicious serving of the doughnut of your choice and my unin-terrupted attention to whatever fascinating topics you care to discuss." I'd been spending too much time with Janine. That speech had sounded exactly like something she would say.

"Cool," Josh said, finally smiling. "Could I carry a few of those books?" He pointed at my stuffed backpack.

"Oh, no, sir! I would be pleased to carry any-thing of your choice." I tugged on the strap of his bag.

"Come on, Claudia," Josh said, laughing. "You're weighed down now. I'll carry my own stuff."

"If you insist." I curtsied.

Josh grabbed my hand and we headed for Donut Express.

We ordered, then found a table in the corner. Josh told me about the report Joanna had given in English class, and I told him how long it had taken to clean up the house after the party. I also thanked him for the vase, and told him how it makes me happy every time I see it.

Things were starting to feel right between us again.

"Claudia!" Kristy and Mary Anne rushed over to our table.

I glanced at Josh. He was watching me, waiting to see what I would do. "Hi, guys," I said. "Don't worry. I'll be on time for the BSC meeting." I looked at Josh, then at the door.

"Sure, we'll see you then," Kristy said, backing away with a puzzled look on her face.

"Hey, Mary Anne, I talked to Logan this morning. We might go bowling together this weekend. He's going to be surprised when he finds out that I'm as good as I said I was," Josh said.

"Logan is pretty good too," Mary Anne replied.

"You and Claudia will have to come along and be our cheerleaders." Josh looked at me.

"Sure. Sounds like fun," I agreed.

"I like to bowl," Kristy put in.

"Maybe we can make a . . ." Josh looked at me, grinning, "party of it."

I groaned. "So long as it's not at my house!"

"I'll check with Stacey, Jessi, Mal, and Abby, if you'll check with Joanna, Shira, and Jeannie," said Kristy.

"You might try to find some time to practice. They call me 'Josh two hundred' around the bowling alleys. I have my own ball. And it has a name."

"You've bowled two hundred?" Mary Anne asked, her eyes growing wide.

"No, but I think by now my total score is at two hundred," Josh said.

We laughed.

Shira waved to us through the window, and Kristy motioned for her to come inside.

"Want to go bowling this weekend?" Josh asked her.

As I watched and listened, I realized that the BSC and my seventh-grade friends would probably never be one big group, but right now they were fitting together pretty well.

Kristy leaned on the back of my chair, her arm resting on my shoulder. Shira knelt on the floor between Josh and me. Mary Anne pulled a chair up to the table and in the tight quarters our knees touched. I reached out and put my hand over Josh's, making the circle complete.

Dear Reader,

In *Claudia's Big Party*, Claudia and Janine are left on their own for a weekend, and Claudia finds that her relationship with her sister is changing. Claudia and Janine have never been close, but now Claudia sees that her sister would like to be her friend too. When I was growing up, I was the big sister like Janine, and Jane was my little sister, like Claudia. We were just two years apart, but for a long time we weren't very close. We had different friends and very different interests. I excelled in school, and my sister excelled in sports and was involved in lots of activities. It was not until we had grown up and each moved to New York City that we became friends and spent a lot of time together. Now my sister is not just my sister, but a mother too, and I have a brand-new nephew Henry, named after our father. Relationships constantly change — so who knows . . . maybe one day Claudia and Janine will be best friends too!

Happy Reading,

Ann M Martin

Ann M. Martin

About the Author

ANN MATTHEWS MARTIN was born on August 12, 1955. She grew up in Princeton, NJ, with her parents and her younger sister, Jane.

Although Ann used to be a teacher and then an editor of children's books, she's now a full-time writer. She gets ideas for her books from many different places. Some are based on personal experiences. Others are based on childhood memories and feelings. Many are written about contemporary problems or events.

All of Ann's characters, even the members of the Baby-sitters Club, are made up. (So is Stoneybrook.) But many of her characters are based on real people. Sometimes Ann names her characters after people she knows, other times she chooses names she likes.

In addition to the Baby-sitters Club books, Ann Martin has written many other books for children. Her favorite is *Ten Kids, No Pets* because she loves big families and she loves animals. Her favorite Baby-sitters Club book is *Kristy's Big Day*. (By the way, Kristy is her favorite baby-sitter!)

Ann M. Martin now lives in New York with her cats, Gussie, Woody, and Willy. Her hobbies are reading, sewing, and needlework — especially making clothes for children.

Notebook Pages

This Baby-sitters Club book belongs to _____Sam_____.

I am ____11____ years old and in the ____5th____ grade.

The name of my school is ____homeschooled____.

I got this BSC book from _____.

I started reading it on _____ and finished reading it on _____.

The place where I read most of this book is _____.

My favorite part was when _____.

If I could change anything in the story, it might be the part when _____

_____

My favorite character in the Baby-sitters Club is _____.

The BSC member I am most like is _____

because _____.

If I could write a Baby-sitters Club book it would be about ____

_____.

#123 Claudia's Big Party

In *Claudia's Big Party*, Claudia gets into big trouble when she throws a party without her parents' permission. The biggest thing I ever did without my parents' permission was _____ _____. One thing I wish my parents would give me permission to do is _____. One thing I don't think my parents will *ever* give me permission to do is _____. Claudia has many different activities planned for her big party. If I were throwing a party, some of the activities would be _____ _____. Some of the people I would invite are _____ _____.

The one room I would make off-limits would be _____ _____.

CLAUDIA'S

a spooky sitting adventure

Finger painting at 3...

Sitting for two of my favorite charges --
Jamie and Lucy Newton.

SCRAPBOOK

...oil painting
at 13!

my family. mom and Dad, me and
Janine... and we'll never forget Mimi.

Interior art by Angelo Tillery

Read all the books
about **Claudia**
in the Baby-sitters Club series
by Ann M. Martin

Mysteries:

Look for #124

STACEY McGILL . . . MATCHMAKER?

Joni turned away from Kristy stubbornly. "I hate Mrs. McGill."

"You wouldn't hate her if you knew her," Kristy said. "And besides, it's just one date. Your dad might date lots of women before he remarries."

"Yuck," Ewan said.

"He might never remarry," Kristy added.

This last statement brightened Joni's outlook a little. "That's true," she admitted hopefully. "He won't ever find another person as good as my mother, no matter how hard he tries."

"Maybe not," Kristy said. "Though, you know, he might find someone he likes in different ways."

"He won't," Joni said confidently.

Although she calmed down at that point,

Joni wasn't as confident as she sounded. Kristy said that no matter how hard she tried to distract the kids with games, videos, and stories, Joni's eyes were glued to the clock. "What's taking him so long?" she wanted to know at only eight o'clock.

Ewan fell asleep at eight-thirty. Joni asked to stay up to read, as she had when I was there, and Kristy said yes. By the time Mr. Brooke returned home at twelve-thirty, Kristy was sure Joni had to be asleep. So she was shocked when Joni appeared on the stairs the moment her father came in. "It's about time!" she scolded him.

Mr. Brooke made light of it, but Kristy said he also seemed a little annoyed with his daughter.

"Stacey," Kristy said to me later, "if your mother sees him again, you're going to have to have a serious talk with those kids. They are not going to make this easy. No way."

I know she was probably right. So I began trying to come up with the best possible words to make this okay for them. It had to be just the right thing. Mr. Brooke wasn't the kind of man I was about to let my mother lose just because his kids were making it hard.

THE BABY-SITTERS CLUB®

Collect 'em all!

100 (and more) Reasons to Stay Friends Forever!

More titles... ▶

The Baby-sitters Club titles continued...

☐ MG22877-3	#93	Mary Anne and the Memory Garden	$3.99
☐ MG22878-1	#94	Stacey McGill, Super Sitter	$3.99
☐ MG22879-X	#95	Kristy + Bart = ?	$3.99
☐ MG22880-3	#96	Abby's Lucky Thirteen	$3.99
☐ MG22881-1	#97	Claudia and the World's Cutest Baby	$3.99
☐ MG22882-X	#98	Dawn and Too Many Sitters	$3.99
☐ MG69205-4	#99	Stacey's Broken Heart	$3.99
☐ MG69206-2	#100	Kristy's Worst Idea	$3.99
☐ MG69207-0	#101	Claudia Kishi, Middle School Dropout	$3.99
☐ MG69208-9	#102	Mary Anne and the Little Princess	$3.99
☐ MG69209-7	#103	Happy Holidays, Jessi	$3.99
☐ MG69210-0	#104	Abby's Twin	$3.99
☐ MG69211-9	#105	Stacey the Math Whiz	$3.99
☐ MG69212-7	#106	Claudia, Queen of the Seventh Grade	$3.99
☐ MG69213-5	#107	Mind Your Own Business, Kristy!	$3.99
☐ MG69214-3	#108	Don't Give Up, Mallory	$3.99
☐ MG69215-1	#109	Mary Anne To the Rescue	$3.99
☐ MG05988-2	#110	Abby the Bad Sport	$3.99
☐ MG05989-0	#111	Stacey's Secret Friend	$3.99
☐ MG05990-4	#112	Kristy and the Sister War	$3.99
☐ MG05911-2	#113	Claudia Makes Up Her Mind	$3.99
☐ MG05911-2	#114	The Secret Life of Mary Anne Spier	$3.99
☐ MG05993-9	#115	Jessi's Big Break	$3.99
☐ MG05994-7	#116	Abby and the Worst Kid Ever	$3.99
☐ MG05995-5	#117	Claudia and the Terrible Truth	$3.99
☐ MG05996-3	#118	Kristy Thomas, Dog Trainer	$3.99
☐ MG05997-1	#119	Stacey's Ex-Boyfriend	$3.99
☐ MG05998-X	#120	Mary Anne and the Playground Fight	$3.99
☐ MG45575-3		Logan's Story Special Edition Readers' Request	$3.25
☐ MG47118-X		Logan Bruno, Boy Baby-sitter Special Edition Readers' Request	$3.50
☐ MG47756-0		Shannon's Story Special Edition	$3.50
☐ MG47686-6		The Baby-sitters Club Guide to Baby-sitting	$3.25
☐ MG47314-X		The Baby-sitters Club Trivia and Puzzle Fun Book	$2.50
☐ MG48400-1		BSC Portrait Collection: Claudia's Book	$3.50
☐ MG22864-1		BSC Portrait Collection: Dawn's Book	$3.50
☐ MG69181-3		BSC Portrait Collection: Kristy's Book	$3.99
☐ MG22865-X		BSC Portrait Collection: Mary Anne's Book	$3.99
☐ MG48399-4		BSC Portrait Collection: Stacey's Book	$3.50
☐ MG92713-2		The Complete Guide to The Baby-sitters Club	$4.95
☐ MG47151-1		The Baby-sitters Club Chain Letter	$14.95
☐ MG48295-5		The Baby-sitters Club Secret Santa	$14.95
☐ MG45074-3		The Baby-sitters Club Notebook	$2.50
☐ MG44783-1		The Baby-sitters Club Postcard Book	$4.95

Available wherever you buy books...or use this order form.

Scholastic Inc., P.O. Box 7502, 2931 E. McCarty Street, Jefferson City, MO 65102

Please send me the books I have checked above. I am enclosing $_____
(please add $2.00 to cover shipping and handling). Send check or money order—
no cash or C.O.D.s please.

Name_____ Birthdate_____

Address _____

City_____ State/Zip _____